## RED CARD
## AGATHA WINNER

The first Zeke Armstrong Mystery, *Red Card,* was the 2003 recipient of the prestigious Agatha Award for Best Children's/Young Adult Mystery.

The Agatha Awards honor traditional mysteries—books best typified by the works of Agatha Christie. The genre is loosely defined as mysteries that contain no gratuitous violence, usually featuring an amateur detective, a confined setting and characters who know one another.

Agatha Awards are nominated by the registered fans and Friends of Malice Domestic at their annual convention in Arlington, Virginia. Winners were selected by all attendees and presented at the Agatha Awards Banquet.

Fifteen years old at the time, coauthor Matthew LaBrot is the youngest-ever recipient of the Agatha Award

# Green Streak

To Daniel's siblings and siblings-in-law,
Don Jr., Bill & Donna, Paul, Kathy & David, and last
but not least, Gale & Don, who are, by some strange
coincidence, Matthew's parents.

## Acknowledgments

Many thanks to Michael & Brenda Harris, and the rest of the Texas Flyers, for the inline skate racing pointers; Stephen Burchill and Nancy Dunnan, for the Manhattan insider information; Jack Robinson, Jeanne Skartsiaris, Danny Bollinger, Alexandra Skartsiaris, and Liam Gartside, for the great input; Geraldine Galentree, for being on our side; Martine Burlinson, for double-checking our French; Jeanne Jew, for the Chinese language help; Fatim Thiam, for unraveling some of the mysteries of Wolof; Bruce Jones, for the virtual skate down a Fifth Avenue sidewalk; Steve Hawthorne, for the geography lesson; Khaled Husseini, for being our eyes in Petra; Jamie Stewart, Neil Barni, Kathy Womble, Tim Chopoorian, Harry Hunsicker, and Drue Gawel, for the fast reads and right-on suggestions; Scott Henry, for keeping a sharp eye out; Martin Rogers and Laurie Baker, for making us look good; Bill Manchee, for taking us into Round Two; PJ Nunn and the gang, for helping us get this far; Dan Silverman, for art's sake, Carol Fass and company, for the good ink; Jane Chelius, for being good at the art of the deal; Lisa Korth, for bringing Zeke into the world; and, finally, Suzanne Frank, Brent Johnson, and Kate Defrise, for years of support and pizza.

# Green Streak

by

Daniel J. Hale
&
Matthew LaBrot

Top Publications, Ltd.
Dallas, Texas

**Green Streak**

A Top Publications Paperback
First Edition
12221 Merit Drive, Suite 750
Dallas, Texas 75251
ALL RIGHTS RESERVED
Copyright 2004
Daniel J. Hale
ISBN#: 1-929976-28-3
Library of Congress # 2003113697

Printed in the United States of America

# Chapter One

It was such a warm and sunny spring morning, I felt like I was skating alongside the Red Sea in Egypt and not The Lake in New York City's Central Park. The wind whistled through my helmet as I zipped down Park Drive. Pow Wow Gao was drafting behind me, the speed making his new five-wheel inline skates sing. The old second-hand pair I wore sounded like they had sand in the bearings. I hoped my wheels would keep rolling long enough for me to finish this qualifying race for tomorrow's Big Apple Inline Skate-Off.

We overtook a pack of the older guys in our age bracket, some of the fifteen-year-olds who hadn't taken that wrong turn early in the race. One of them, a guy with a camouflage shirt and a fake rhinoceros horn glued to the front of his helmet, shouted rude names as we passed. He obviously didn't like the fact that a couple of thirteen-year-olds were going to cross the finish line before he did.

Pow Wow called out, "Good pull, Zeke!"

He and I had skated fast to recover from our mistake, but I knew we'd have to pass eight or nine more guys in our age group if we were going to qualify. Competing in tomorrow's race meant a lot to me, but I knew it meant even more to Pow Wow. Inline skate racing was one of his best sports.

We rounded the curve at the southern tip of The Lake. A woman who looked to be the same age as Pow Wow's mom passed us like we were standing still. That was what Uncle Dane would call a "humbling experience." As she zipped ahead, I saw the exit sign for West 72nd Street. Park Drive would soon veer left and begin its final uphill ascent. The grade wasn't very steep, but it would be a long climb to the top. After that, a quick downhill would take us to the finish line.

Even though Pow Wow was usually a faster skater than I was, he'd just gotten over a bad case of the flu. He was still weak. I knew he had to be tired. I certainly was. I didn't know how much either of us had left to give. However much that was, we had to give it now – the race was almost over.

I spotted another pack of skaters ahead on Park Drive. There were half a dozen of them. All were fourteen- and fifteen-year-old guys. They weren't skating as fast as we were. If Pow Wow and I could maintain our speed up the hill, we'd be able to pass them. After that, we'd only have to overtake three or four more of the guys in our age bracket.

If they hadn't already crossed the finish line, that is.

When I looked back to tell Pow Wow to pour it on, I noticed that he'd fallen behind. His face was red, his light-gray shirt was dark with sweat. He didn't look so good.

I called out, "You okay?"

He nodded.

We were no longer gaining on the pack of skaters uphill. I called back to Pow Wow, "It's not much further."

Even as I said that, I wondered if it was any use to try.

Any of our earlier practice runs around Central Park's Outer Loop would have easily qualified us for the race. Today, though, we had made the mistake of following a group of skaters who took a wrong turn at East 72$^{nd}$ Street. For some reason, there weren't any race officials at the intersection. Pow Wow and I were so focused on passing the pack that we didn't realize we were going the wrong way until the guys started turning around. That error cost us a lot of time.

Even so, we were now just minutes from the finish line. We might not qualify, but it made no sense to give up so far into the race. We *had* to try.

As I glanced back to see Pow Wow moving back into drafting position, I noticed a tall, lean man dressed in green pants and a long-sleeved green shirt. He was zigzagging through the pack of fifteen-year-olds we had just passed. The mirror-green lenses of his sports sunglasses were huge – they covered most of his face. There was something in the way the tall man in green was skating. It almost seemed as if he were racing for his life.

Pow Wow and I would have to do the same if we were going to qualify for tomorrow's big race.

I took it up a notch. A crash came from behind. I was afraid I'd pulled Pow Wow too hard and caused him to wipe out. When I looked over my shoulder, though, I saw that he was still gaining on me.

Further back, the fast man in green had collided with the guy in the rhinoceros-horn helmet and the camouflage shirt. Both were down. I hoped neither of them had gotten hurt. Even if that were the case, though, the officials would take care of them. It was in the race rules. My job was to qualify.

Pow Wow's wheels hummed as he pulled into formation behind me. We quickly outpaced the first five guys in the pack. The one in the front, though, began to pick up speed. I didn't think I had any more in me, but somehow I was able to skate even harder. Slowly but surely, Pow Wow and I managed to pass him, too.

Atop the hill, we once again passed the big statue of Giuseppe Mazzini. For the fifth time in three days, I wondered who Giuseppe Mazzini was and why there was a monument to him in Central Park. Next time I was in a library, I thought, I'd have to look him up.

The thought didn't last long.

At the bottom of the hill was the finish line. Crowds bulged out on both sides of the wide stripe of red paint. There were about ten skaters between us and that line. Three of them were in our age group. All three were within striking distance.

My legs were like rubber. No matter how good it would feel to stand there and let gravity pull me down the hill, I knew that wouldn't be enough to qualify. I kept pumping. On the downhill, my speed quickly increased. The air cut through my sweaty shirt. My skates sounded like they were on the verge of disintegrating. As I passed Tavern on the Green – Mrs. Gao's dream restaurant – Pow Wow pulled up beside me.

"You okay?" I asked.

With a sudden burst of speed, he pulled ahead and shouted, "Come on, slowpoke!"

I caught up quickly. Side-by-side, Pow Wow and I skated down the hill. We were going fast, dangerously fast. I knew that if either of us wiped out at that speed, we would be injured pretty badly. I didn't want to break a leg and spend six weeks hobbling around on crutches, like Pow Wow's dad. I just hoped my skates would hold together, and that we could avoid the rocks, sticks, and other debris on the road.

A third of the way down the slope, Pow Wow and I passed the first of the remaining skaters in our age bracket. As I set my sights on the other two, I caught a glimpse of someone coming up fast from behind.

The man in green who'd collided with the rhino-horn guy streaked past us. With the exception of his black, five-wheel skates, everything he wore was green. Even his strange-looking helmet was green. There was no race number on the side of his pants. I guessed that it had fallen off during the crash at the bottom of the hill. He rushed headlong down the slope. As he blew past the two remaining guys in our bracket, one of them looked back and saw Pow Wow and me gaining on them.

The guys sped up. Pow Wow and I were running out of space and time. I was so focused on it that I almost didn't notice the small black object rolling down the road ahead of me. I straddled it in the nick of time. It was an inline skate wheel. I wondered for a moment if it had come from my skate, but that would have been impossible. It must have come from one of the other racers downhill.

Pow Wow moved up beside me. We glanced at each other, then we both gave it every last ounce of energy we had. Moments after we passed the last two skaters in our bracket, the red line blurred under our feet. Just like that, the qualifying race was over.

Pow Wow and I slowed ourselves on the level road and circled back. We had skated faster today than we ever had skated before. Even so, I didn't know if our speed at the end had been enough to make up for our mistake early in the race. We went to the refreshment table, grabbed the last two cups of sports drink on the table, and chugged them down. We threw the paper cups in the trash and walked away.

Between breaths, Pow Wow said, "Do you think we qualified?"

I shook my head. "I don't know. That wrong turn may have cost us too much time."

"Richard! Zeke!"

We turned to see the Gaos approaching through the crowd. Mrs. Gao was carrying our bulky sports bags. Dr. Gao was hobbling along on his crutches.

On the very first run of a ski trip we'd taken to Colorado last month, Dr. and Mrs. Gao, Uncle Dane, and Courtney – Uncle Dane's girlfriend – had taken the express aerial tram to the top of the mountain. There was no way anyone was going to get me in one of those things – gondolas were my worst nightmare – so Pow Wow rode the chairlift with me. Along the way, he asked why I could ride an open ski lift and not the gondola, since they were both suspended from a cable. I didn't have an answer. I just knew that I was okay outside and not okay inside. When we were halfway to the top, Uncle Dane's voice came over the two-way radio we used while skiing. After Dr. Gao had gotten out of the gondola, before he'd even stepped into his skis, he'd slipped on a patch of compacted snow and broken his leg.

When Mrs. Gao reached us, it looked as if she might try to hug Pow Wow and me. Seeing how sweaty we were, though, she just patted our shoulders. Dr. Gao hobbled over, pushed his glasses up higher on his nose, then shook our hands. "Good job, guys!"

Even though both of Pow Wow's parents were born in mainland China, they had moved to the United States when they were children. Their English was perfect and their accents were American. Pow Wow hadn't even learned Chinese. Dr. Gao was an emergency room physician. Mrs. Gao had been a nurse. They met at a hospital in San Francisco where they both had worked. Dr. Gao would be attending a medical conference – the same one my dad was attending – here in New York starting the day after tomorrow. Dr. and Mrs. Gao had been nice enough to bring Pow Wow and me to New York a few days early so we could compete in the Big Apple Inline Skate-Off.

As the Gaos began to discuss where we would go for lunch, I noticed the Green Man again. Even with the large, reflective lenses of his sports sunglasses, I could tell that he was nervous. His head jerked from side to side as he scanned the crowd. It looked like he was trying to find someone. I wondered why he was so jittery.

A woman in a daisy-print dress walked past and approached a big bulletin board that had been set up near the drink table. She began to tack sheets of white paper to the board. I exchanged glances with Pow Wow and his parents, then I hurried over to where she stood. A crowd filled in behind me.

When I finally found the sheet for our age bracket, I started scanning the columns from the top. Then, I thought, it would make more sense to start at the bottom. The last name listed was "Armstrong, Zeke." Just above my name was "Gao, Richard."

Pow Wow and I were the last two qualifiers!

After scanning the rest of the qualifiers in our age group to see what our competition would be like,

I made my way back through the crowd, found Pow Wow, and gave him the news. I started breaking down the leaders and the other qualifiers by time. Dr. and Mrs. Gao gave each other strange looks.

Pow Wow laughed and said, "The kids at school call him RAM."

I rolled my eyes.

Mrs. Gao gave a thin smile. "You mean, like a goat?"

Pow Wow laughed again. "You know how computers have RAM—random access memory?"

The Gaos nodded.

"Well, Zeke has Random *Armstrong* Memory."

I frowned and shook my head.

Mrs. Gao said, "You should be proud of that, Zeke. I have a hard time remembering my own phone number."

"Speaking of phones…" Dr. Gao passed me the mobile unit Uncle Dane had me carry whenever we were apart. "Your uncle called."

As I was walking away from the noise of the crowd, I caught another glimpse of the Jittery Green Man. He was skating along slowly, his head jerking this way and that as he moved through the clusters of people. If he were looking for someone, it didn't seem to me that he was looking for a friend.

# Chapter Two

I left my uncle a voice mail message giving him news of how Pow Wow and I had qualified for the Big Apple Inline Skate-Off. Uncle Dane was in Los Angeles today, but this evening he'd be taking the red-eye—a flight leaving California late tonight and arriving in New York early tomorrow morning. Since his interview with *The New York Times* was scheduled for late tomorrow afternoon, he'd be able to watch Pow Wow and me race in the morning.

I clipped the phone to the waistband of my shorts and headed back to where the Gaos were waiting. As I drew near, though, I could see that they were having what looked like a private conversation.

I decided to stop and wait until they finished their family talk.

My own parents would be arriving tomorrow for the medical conference. I could hardly wait to see them. Like Dr. Gao, my dad's a physician. Mom's an architect – she designs buildings. My folks are members of Health for the World, an international organization that builds hospitals and clinics in remote areas with poor medical care. When they left Peru to move to India, I went to Dallas to live with my dad's brother, Dane Armstrong.

I like Uncle Dane. Even though he passes out a lot of what he calls "pearls of wisdom," he's a lot of fun. With the exception of some of his ex-girlfriends, pretty much everyone likes Uncle Dane. He writes suspense novels for adults.

What most people don't know is that Uncle Dane also writes the *Ezekiel Tobias* kids' books under a pen name – Abraham Grey. Even fewer people know that the *Ezekiel Tobias* books are about *me*. I'd like to keep it that way. It seems that wherever my parents and I went – we lived in seven different countries before I came to Dallas – I managed to stumble into some pretty dangerous situations. That's why Mom and Dad sent me to live with Uncle Dane – they thought it would be safer for me. So far, that hasn't been the case.

Mrs. Gao looked at me, smiled, and waved me over.

As I walked toward the Gaos, I thought about my parents. Even though I saw them every three or four months, I wanted to spend more time with them. As it turned out, my wish might come true. Health for the World was having trouble raising money. If it couldn't find new funding soon, Mom and Dad would have to move to Dallas. I loved the thought of living with them again, but it was hard to imagine them not being able to continue the work that was so important to them. Besides that, I think it would be hard for them to live in any one place more than two years.

When I reached the Gaos, Pow Wow's dad said we should drink plenty of liquids since it was such a warm day and we'd had a hard workout. We told him that they had run out of sports drink for the racers.

Pow Wow's mom said, "I should have brought water for you boys." She shook her head. "I'm a terrible mother."

Dr. Gao braced himself on his crutches, passed Pow Wow some money, then put his arm around Mrs. Gao. "You guys go get yourselves something to drink." With a wink and a smile, he pointed out an empty park bench and said, "Richard's terrible mother and I will camp out over there."

I told Dr. Gao that I had some money in my pocket, but he just smiled and told me to save it.

Pow Wow and I decided to go to the window-service café we'd seen on the north side of the ball fields the day before. As we skated along the path that skirted one of the baseball diamonds, we came up behind a woman walking a big, white, shaggy dog.

I whispered to Pow Wow, "That pooch looks like he's wearing a flokati."

He scrunched up his face. "What's a flokati?"

"A kind of rug they make in Greece." I glanced ahead. "Imagine that mutt lying down flat on a floor."

Pow Wow laughed as we passed the woman and the flokati dog.

As we neared the café, I noticed the Jittery Green Man again. He was several yards ahead of us. Even though he skated at a slow pace, as if he wasn't in a hurry, his head was still jerking from side to side. I wondered what he was so nervous about.

Something in my gut told me to stay away from him, so I slowed down to match his speed and keep my distance. Pow Wow asked why I was going so slow. I didn't want to tell him that I thought the Jittery Green Man was up to no good. It had been a couple of weeks since he called me "Sherlock" – as in Sherlock Holmes – and I wanted to keep it that way. I told Pow Wow that I was tired from the race. It wasn't the real reason, but at least it was the truth.

The Jittery Green Man kept moving when we reached the café. That was a relief. The line from the café window stretched all the way out to the path. Pow Wow and I skated to the end of it and waited. After three or four minutes, the line didn't move at all.

Pow Wow said, "This is going to take forever."

I nodded. "I think there's a concession stand near the merry-go-round. Let's go there."

We continued along the path. Central Park was filled with big trees and rolling green hills and huge lumps of dark rock sticking up out of the ground. Squirrels scurried across the grass. Birds circled overhead. It was strange seeing so much nature in the middle of such a huge city.

Pow Wow and I skated alongside an antique carousel spinning around inside an old brick structure. The air was filled with music from a time when my grandparents had been younger than me. Children rode on colorfully painted horses that rose and fell as they swirled past. The parents of some of the older kids watched the merry-go-round through a decorated iron fence.

The concession stand was near the merry-go-round's entrance. Two well-dressed women with long blond hair were talking to the man behind the counter. An elderly, gray-haired woman wearing horn-rimmed glasses and a dark-blue dress with white polka-dots on it stood behind them. A white leather purse hung from her arm.

Pow Wow and I got in line behind the older woman. Her dress was clean and pressed, but it looked a bit old and was almost threadbare at the elbows. She smelled like talcum powder.

After our workout, Pow Wow and I probably weren't smelling very sweet. I wondered if our body odor might make the lady sick. I skated backwards a bit, just to give her some breathing room.

As I did that, the lady turned and looked at me. Her jaw dropped slightly. She then turned and faced forward.

Pow Wow said, "Can you believe it, Zeke? Even after that wrong turn, we actually qualified for the race!"

The elderly woman turned and looked at me again. This time, though, she kept staring.

Not knowing what else to do, I smiled and said, "Hi."

"I'm sorry." The lady smiled weakly. "Did he say your name was Pete?"

I shook my head then stuck out my hand, the way my dad or Uncle Dane would, and said, "I'm Zeke."

With a smile, she took my hand. "You can call me Ms. Nattie. It's a pleasure to meet you, Zeke." Her hands were rough, as if she worked with them a lot.

When I introduced her to Pow Wow, I called him Richard. It was always easier than explaining how he got his nickname.

Ms. Nattie shook Pow Wow's hand. The only jewelry she wore was a thin, pink-gold band on the ring finger of her left hand. She then looked at me and said, "You must think me a strange old bird for staring. It's just that you look a lot like my son."

*Her son?* I wondered if she might be a bit too old to have a boy my age.

Ms. Nattie smiled again. "What I mean is, you look like what my son looked like at your age. His name's Pete." She then gave a long stare. "You be sure to stay away from abandoned refrigerators, alright?"

*What a strange thing for her to say.* I didn't how to reply to that, so I just nodded.

"I have a grandson – Nick. He's about your age. What are you boys? Twelve? Thirteen?"

Pow Wow and I spoke at the same time. "Thirteen."

"Then he's exactly your age." Ms. Nattie looked at me, cocked her head to the side, then added, "My son's wife, Nick's mom, is from India, so Nick doesn't look so much like you, Zeke."

I still didn't know what to say to that, either, so I nodded again.

Ms. Nattie glanced at the race numbers on the sides of our shorts, then down at our feet. "Nick's a big skater. He races in the Skate-Off every year. The three of you would have been in the same age bracket."

Pow Wow asked, "He's not here?"

Ms. Nattie shook her head. "He's spending a month in India with his parents. His mom's younger brother just got married. They'll be home in three days."

I thought about mentioning that my parents were living in India, but decided against it. Anytime I said anything about it, the conversation always got to be long and drawn-out. I didn't really mind that, but sometimes people would put two and two together and figure out that I was the real Ezekiel Tobias. I wanted to keep my secret whenever I could.

Ms. Nattie smiled. "Richard, Zeke, may I buy you boys a lemonade?"

From the look of her dress, I wondered if Ms. Nattie could afford to do that, so I thanked her for offering but told her that she didn't have to do that. Pow Wow told her that his dad had given us money. I told her I had some, too.

Ms. Nattie said, "Keep your money, boys. I'm paying, and I won't take no for an answer." She ordered three lemonades – one without ice – then opened her white leather purse and pulled out a big roll of money.

As soon as I saw the wad of bills, I thought of something Uncle Dane would say: *You can't judge a book by its cover.*

Ms. Nattie peeled off one of the bills, paid the man behind the counter, then dropped the change into her handbag. The concession man handed us three paper cups. Pow Wow and I took ours, which were loaded with ice, and thanked Ms. Nattie. As the three of us walked away, I heard a ringing sound.

At first, I thought it was my mobile phone. When I unclipped it from my waistband, though, I found it wasn't ringing.

"Oh, dear. Would you hold this, Zeke?" Ms. Nattie passed me her lemonade and opened her purse. She reached inside, pulled out a disc-shaped metallic device, then pushed a button which silenced the alarm. She smiled. "Time and numbers – I can't keep track of either."

Pow Wow looked like he was going to make another Random Armstrong Memory comment, but I gave him my *You better not* look. He didn't say a word.

Ms. Nattie reached into her purse again, fished out a medication bottle, opened it, shook out a capsule, then returned the bottle to her handbag. She pulled the capsule apart, emptied the powdered contents into her lemonade, then took the cup from me. She smiled and said, "I have a hard time swallowing pills."

As she took a sip, Pow Wow asked, "Are you sick?"

I elbowed him and whispered, "Pow Wow! That's not very nice."

"That's alright, Zeke" said Ms. Nattie. "Yes, Richard, I am sick. But as long as I take my medicine every eight hours, I'll be fine. Like I said, I'm bad with time and numbers. That's why I have the medication alarm."

Pow Wow and I talked to Ms. Nattie for several minutes. She was a really nice lady. She told us some interesting stories from when she was as girl growing up on Roosevelt Island, which she said had once been called Welfare Island. I especially liked hearing about her playing in the tunnels that the nurses would use when they had to walk to the hospital in the winter.

The Gaos had taken Pow Wow and me on a boat tour around Manhattan the afternoon we arrived. All along the way, Mrs. Gao read aloud some "interesting tidbits" from *New York Now!*, a guide book that she'd bought in Dallas. When we passed between Roosevelt Island and the Island of Manhattan, she started reciting the section about the Roosevelt Island Tram, the aerial cable car that connected the two islands. Chills ran down my spine. I couldn't stand the thought of being in an enclosed gondola. My whole family had missed seeing the view from the top of Table Mountain in South Africa because Mom and Dad couldn't get me to ride the aerial tram. I was just glad that Roosevelt Island – if I ever visited it – could be reached by bridge and subway.

All of a sudden, I thought about the Gaos. They were waiting for us. Pow Wow and I shook Ms. Nattie's rough hand and said goodbye. She told us once more to stay out of abandoned refrigerators, then she walked away toward a tunnel, near which was a sign marked "Playmates Arch."

As Pow Wow and I began skating back to where his parents were waiting, he said, "Ms. Nattie's a neat old lady, but what's with the refrigerators?"

"I'm not sure. Uncle Dane said that back in the old days, kids would sometimes get–"

My words were cut short when a man on inline skates zoomed past. He almost knocked the lemonade out of my hand. He was moving so fast, it appeared as if he were little more than a streak. A *green* streak.

*Oh, no!*

I spun around to see that the Jittery Green Man was heading straight for Ms. Nattie.

I yelled, "Ms. Nattie!"

She looked back.

It was too late.

The Jittery Green Man grabbed her white purse. As he yanked it out of her hand, Ms. Nattie began to fall. She looked like a statue tipping over in slow motion. The Jittery Green Man slowed and looked back. When she hit the ground, he came to a quick stop. For a moment, it looked like he might come back to try to help her. Then, he turned and. zoomed away through the Playmates Arch tunnel.

## Chapter Three

I had started skating toward Ms. Nattie before the Jittery Green Man snatched her purse. It seemed to take forever to get there. I skidded into a hockey stop—I'd never before been able to do a hockey stop on five-wheel skates—and knelt at her side. Her eyes were closed. The frames of her horn-rim glasses were broken, but at least the lenses hadn't shattered. There was no blood that I could see. Her cup of lemonade, the lemonade in which she had dissolved her medication, lay spilt across the pavement. I called out, "Ms. Nattie?"

There was no reply. She didn't move. I felt for a pulse. Her heartbeat seemed strong. She was still breathing, but she had hit her head on the pavement. She'd been knocked unconscious.

Pow Wow skated up beside me.

I unclipped the mobile phone from the waistband of my shorts and pitched it to him. "Call 9-1-1, then call your dad. Don't let anyone move her until medical help arrives." I stood and hurried away.

Pow Wow called out to me. "What are you doing?"

As I skated away, I yelled over my shoulder. "Going to get her medication!" There was no time to explain, but Pow Wow was a smart guy. I knew he'd figure out why it was so important that I get her capsules.

Ms. Nattie never told us her last name. She wasn't wearing a medical alert bracelet. All of her identification was most likely in her purse. We had no idea who she was. Since my dad was a doctor, I knew it might be a long time – hours, even days – before she woke up. Until then, she wouldn't be able to tell the doctors in the emergency room what sort of medication she needed. She'd only had a sip or two of her lemonade before she fell. Almost all of the dose she was supposed to have taken was now spilled across the pavement. I didn't know how much time she'd have to get the rest of the medication into her system, but I couldn't risk waiting.

I skated under the Playmates Arch. The tunnel smelled like the men's room in one of those rest areas on the interstate. I could hear Pow Wow shouting his location into my mobile phone. My skates were making a screeching sound that echoed from the red-and-white brick roof. I hoped the wheels wouldn't lock up before I could get Ms. Nattie's purse.

What I was doing might have been a little risky. Even so, it wasn't like I was trying to chase down the Jittery Green Man and tackle him to the ground. That would have been stupid. The guy was a lot bigger than me, and for all I knew he might have been carrying a knife or a gun. If things went the way I thought they would, I'd never have to go anywhere near the Jittery Green Man.

Uncle Dane had put a mugging in his latest book. While doing research, he told that purse snatchers often ditched handbags after they'd taken the cash, jewelry, and other valuables. Chances were, the Jittery Green Man would grab that wad of money then throw away Ms. Nattie's purse. Until he did that, all I had to do was keep a safe distance and keep him in sight.

To keep him in sight, though, I first had to *get* him in sight.

After clearing the Playmates Arch tunnel, I skated up the slope on the other side. As I climbed, I kept a lookout for the Jittery Green Man in case he was hiding behind a rock or a tree or in the bushes. When I reached the top of the hill, I saw the Dairy just ahead. Several inline skaters milled about on the walkway that ran beneath the porch in front of the old Dairy building. None of them were wearing green.

I felt helpless. Ms. Nattie might not survive if I couldn't get her medication. *What am I supposed to do?*

Just then, something glinting in the sun caught the corner of my eye. I looked down to see a pair of sports sunglasses with green, mirrored lenses lying in the grass. Nearby lay two green shirts. I slowed and looked more closely. What I saw wasn't two green shirts. I was looking at two *halves* of a green shirt, the front and the back.

I wondered if maybe...

I kept moving ahead. As I skated onto the Dairy porch, I saw two halves of a pair of green pants lying underneath a bench. Just ahead, a single, small piece of green cloth was draped across the railing on the edge of the porch.

Uncle Dane's girlfriend, Courtney Bond, was an actress. They met when she came to Dallas to help out the local theatre where she'd gotten her start. Courtney took me backstage once and showed me some of the performers' tricks. The clothes the Jittery Green Man had worn were the breakaway type used for making quick costume changes. It only took a moment for me to figure out that the smaller piece of cloth must have covered the Jittery Green Man's helmet.

Strange, I thought. *Why would anyone go to so much trouble to get away from a mugging?* There was no time to figure that out, though. I had to find the Jittery Green Man. Instead of a man in green, though, I was now looking for a man *not* in green.

On the pathway ahead, I saw three people on inline skates. One was a short woman dressed all in black. The other two were men. Both were tall, both had black, five-wheel skates on their feet.

The first of the men wore black shorts, a black T-shirt and an orange helmet. His clothes were neat in appearance. A large black backpack was slung over his shoulder.

The other man was dressed in frayed, cut-off denim shorts and a ripped T-shirt. He wore an old-fashioned white helmet. He was holding something against his chest, but I couldn't see what it was. *Ms. Nattie's purse?*

At Park Drive, the neatly dressed man turned right and headed south. The ragged man veered to the left. Though something told me the ragged man was too obvious, I knew the Jittery Green Man hadn't been carrying a backpack during the race. Besides, the neatly dressed man looked too normal to be a purse-snatcher.

I fixed my sights on the man in the ragged clothes and prepared to follow him. Just as I reached Park Drive, though, I noticed something important: The neatly dressed man's left skate was missing one of its wheels. I flashed back to the final downhill portion of that morning's qualifying race and remembered the wheel I'd had to avoid.

Could it have come from the Jittery Green Man's skate?

I looked at the ragged man again. Although I only caught a peek of what he was clutching to his chest, I could see that it was small, white, and furry. He was holding a kitten or a puppy or some other small animal. Whatever it was, it *wasn't* a purse.

At the last possible moment, I peeled off to the right.

I slowed myself and matched the neatly dressed man's speed. He didn't seem to notice me following him, so I tried to blend in with the other skaters on the path. I reminded myself that all I had to do was watch until he ditched Ms. Nattie's purse, which I hoped to be the bulge in his backpack.

I wondered where he'd gotten the backpack. He must have stashed it somewhere along the trail then retrieved it when he'd shed his green clothes. Either that, or he'd been wearing it flat against his back beneath his breakaway shirt.

Again I wondered why someone would go through so much trouble just to make a clean getaway from a mugging. I thought of how the Jittery Green Man seemed to have been searching for someone at the end of the race. I remembered how he'd been skating alongside the ball fields trying to act casual. Taking into account his breakaway green clothing and the hidden backpack, it all seemed to add up to one thing: The Jittery Green Man had hunted down Ms. Nattie. I just couldn't figure out why.

Right now, though, that wasn't important. I had to figure out how to follow the Jittery Green Man – no longer wearing green – without his knowing I was following him. He may have seen me talking to Ms. Nattie.

The Jittery Green Man had changed his appearance. I needed to do the same thing. I needed a disguise. In *Ezekiel Tobias and the Lost Inca Gold*, Uncle Dane wrote about the native Peruvian costume I'd worn to fool the tomb robbers. Of course, a get-up like that would call a lot of attention to me now. What I needed was another sort of disguise, something that would let me blend in with the crowd in Central Park.

When I looked down at my clothes, I noticed my race number attached to the side of my shorts. I yanked it off and threw it into a trash can as I skated past. My tank top was reversible. I quickly pulled it off, turned it inside-out, then put it back on. Now, instead of a royal-blue shirt, I was wearing a bright-yellow one. The problem was, my helmet was an even brighter shade of yellow. The thing practically glowed in the dark.

My parents and Uncle Dane were always preaching the dangers of not wearing protective headgear. It was probably illegal to skate without a helmet in New York City. Even so, getting rid of it seemed the only thing I could to do change my appearance enough so that the Jittery Man wouldn't recognize me. My safety was important, but was Ms. Nattie's life less important? I thought not. Besides, if a policeman stopped me for a safety violation, I could point out the Jittery Man and have him arrested.

I took off my helmet and tossed it onto the grass near a big black boulder. My hair was a mess, but it was so sweaty that I didn't have to worry about the cowlick that always seemed to crop up on top of my mop of brown hair. Cowlick or no, I hoped I wouldn't fall and fracture my skull before I could get my hands on Ms. Nattie's medication.

# Chapter Four

When he came to the end of Park Drive, the Jittery Man crossed a circular drive jammed with yellow cabs then skated onto a crowded plaza. I dodged a moving taxi as I followed him.

In the center of the plaza stood a shiny gold statue of a man on a horse. The name on the statue's base was William Tecumseh Sherman, the American Civil War general. The Plaza Hotel was ahead and to the right. The Sherry-Netherland was off to the left. I knew the two hotels because Uncle Dane and I had been guests at both…when his publisher was paying for the rooms. Otherwise, we would stay at his university club in Midtown.

I didn't need to look at a street sign to know where we were – 60th Street and Fifth Avenue. Street performers entertained the tourists. Horse-drawn carriages clip-clopped past toward 59<sup>th</sup>. Cars blared down Fifth. There were no policemen in sight.

The Jittery Man skated over to Fifth Avenue and held up his hand. He was hailing a cab. I had enough money in my pocket to take a taxi just about anywhere in the city.

Within moments, a cab stopped and the Jittery Man jumped in.

I quickly skated over to Fifth, held up my hand, and screamed, "Taxi!" A yellow cab pulled up at the curb. I opened the back door and half-tripped inside. Feeling like a character in an old movie, I said, "Follow that cab!"

I expected the taxi driver – a tall, lean man with very dark skin and even darker hair and eyes – to tell me to get out of his taxi. Instead, he accelerated away from the curb.

Soon, we were heading south on Fifth Avenue directly behind the Jittery Man's taxi. My cabbie pointed at it and, in a thick French accent, said, "Zis one?"

"Yes, sir."

Several blocks later, the Jittery Man's cab turned left. My taxi followed. We drove into the shadows of the city canyon.

As we made our way between mountains of glass, steel, brick, and concrete, I had a thought. I tapped on the Plexiglas separating me from the driver and, speaking through the holes punched in it, asked, "Can you call the police from your taxi?"

The cabbie glanced back at me. "Why?"

I pointed ahead. "The man riding in the back of that taxi. He stole a lady's purse. Her medicine is in the purse. She'll die without it."

The cab in which I was riding braked to a halt at a stoplight, and the driver turned to look me in the eye. "You do not lie?"

"No, sir." I didn't bat an eye. Uncle Dane had told me that people blinked when they were lying. "I'm telling the truth."

The cabbie obviously believed me, because he picked up the microphone of his radio. He spoke in

French and in Wolof, an African tribal language. My parents and I had spent some time in Senegal, the farthest western country in Africa. They spoke Wolof there. I couldn't make out everything the cabbie said in Wolof, but he spoke enough in French for me to know that he was asking the man on the radio to call the police. The cabbie gave his own taxi's number, then the number and license plate of the cab in front of us.

As we drove ahead, I thought of the months my parents and I had spent in Dakar – Senegal's capital – while waiting for the political situation in a neighboring country to become less dangerous. Dakar's a nice city. It's like Paris with palm trees and a beach. While we were there, we met some men who worked for the United States Meteorological Society. They were studying strong weather patterns. One of them told me that those weather patterns sometimes resulted in the hurricanes that reached the United States.

The taxi in which I was riding came to a stop at a red light. The Jittery Man's cab was just ahead. I looked around wondering where the police could be. I wished they would hurry.

When the traffic signal turned green, the Jittery Man's taxi lurched forward. The cab in which I was riding quickly followed. On the far side of the intersection, though, we came to a sudden stop. Something had stopped the traffic ahead.

As I looked ahead to see if it was the police who had blocked off the street, the rear door of the cab in front flew open. The Jittery Man jumped out. He was wearing a red sweatshirt, a red baseball cap, and a pair of gold-tinted wrap-around sunglasses. I wondered how he'd fit all the extra items into his backpack. He slung the pack over his right shoulder then glanced back, to check for traffic I guessed. I tried to get a better look at him. The large gold-mirror lenses of his glasses covered a lot of his face. It was still hard to tell what he looked like. He turned and ran down the sidewalk. He was no longer on skates. Instead, he wore a pair of white sneakers.

There was no time to think, only to act. Even though there was a chance that the Jittery Man had left Ms. Nattie's purse in the cab, something told me he still had it in the backpack. I memorized the license plate of the Jittery Man's cab as well as the number of the taxi in which I was riding. I opened the back door and said, "*Désolé, monsieur. Je vous payerai bientôt. C'est promis.*"

The cabbie didn't say a word as I skated away.

# Chapter Five

Men, women, children, and dogs filled the sidewalk. As soon as I skated into the crowd, I could no longer see the Jittery Man. With the bright-red baseball cap he wore, it should have been easy to keep him in sight. *Where did he go?*

I'd heard Uncle Dane say on more than one occasion that when your brain didn't tell you what to do, you had to rely on your instincts. That was his way of saying, "Trust your gut." My gut was telling me to keep moving forward.

The sky was clear-blue, and the sun was shining, but the tall buildings cast dark shadows over the sidewalk. I thought about the time my parents took me to see Petra, in southern Jordan. To reach the city of ancient buildings carved into solid rock, we had to walk through a slot canyon, a narrow valley with tall, vertical sandstone walls. The locals called it a "*siq*." Even on that bright, sunny morning, it had felt like late afternoon in the shade of the canyon. This Manhattan sidewalk reminded me of that.

I skated through the crowd, careful not to get tangled in a dog leash, or knock down a little kid, or run over anyone's toes. There was no sign of the Jittery Man. Just as I was on the verge of panicking, I saw a red baseball cap rounding the corner. I first checked for traffic, then I jumped down onto the street and skated up the edge of the crowd toward the corner. I did a T-stop just before I reached the intersection.

When I peered around the edge of the building, I saw the Jittery Man duck into a doorway halfway down the block. I quickly skated up the sidewalk then slowed to a crawl when I neared the building I thought the Jittery Man had entered. The street-level windows were covered with large sheets of plywood. It looked like the place was closed for renovations. I figured that I must have estimated wrong, that the Jittery Man had gone into some other building.

As I rolled past a gap in two pieces of the plywood, though, I caught a glimpse of a well-lit room. Inside were two men. One of them was wearing a red shirt.

I skated several yards down the block then stopped. What was I going to do? Snooping around that building would be dangerous. Even so, Ms. Nattie needed my help. I decided to take what Uncle Dane would call a "calculated risk."

When I neared the gap between the sheets of plywood, I stopped and dropped down on one knee. The bottom of the window was about three feet off the ground. I leaned forward and looked in.

The two men had their backs turned toward me. One was an athletic-looking white man with buzz-cut blond hair. Even though he had taken off his baseball cap, he still wore the red sweatshirt. I knew it was the Jittery Man. The other man was also Caucasian, but he appeared older and out of shape. His long black hair looked dirty and greasy.

The Jittery Man and the Greasy Man were standing in a room with ragged walls. Overhead hung a single, bare light bulb. Between the men was a round, waist-high table, the kind you might see in the entryway of a wealthy person's house. On the table there was a pile of items and…Ms. Nattie's purse!

I looked around. The sidewalk was empty. There were no police cars on the street. I thought about going to find a payphone, or perhaps walking into an office building and asking someone there to call the police. The problem was, most offices were closed today, and if I went to find a payphone, the Jittery Man and the Greasy Man might leave. If they took the capsules, Ms. Nattie could be in big trouble.

I was going to have to take back her medication bottle.

The door that led into the building was also boarded over. I eased over to it and pushed, gently. It wouldn't budge. I tried pulling. The door opened without a sound. I half-cringed as I looked inside. I was relieved to see that the room in which the Jittery

Man and the Greasy Man were standing was behind a closed door.

I rolled inside and let the street door close behind me. The corridor in which I found myself had peeling paint on the walls and a dirty concrete floor. At the far end of the hallway burned a single fluorescent light. There was a large gap at the bottom of the door that led into the room occupied by the Jittery Man and the Greasy Man.

I heard a voice. A man's voice. I got down on my hands and knees, crawled over to the gap, and peeked under the door. I saw the base of the table and two pairs of shoes – sneakers and worn brown loafers. The Jittery Man was wearing the tennis shoes – I remembered that from when he stepped out of the cab. That meant that the loafers belonged to the Greasy Man.

A male voice floated underneath the doorway. It sounded like only one of the men was talking. All at once, the voice shouted, "I don't care if the old bat got hurt. That's not our problem."

There was a space of silence.

The same voice spoke again. "If you didn't have the stomach for the job, you shouldn't have come along." From the way the worn brown loafers were moving, I thought it must be the Greasy Man doing all the talking. He spoke in English, but he had a strange accent. It could have been Dutch or German.

The Jittery Man said nothing.

"Can't you do anything right?" The Greasy Man yelled, "It *has* to be here. You're obviously looking in the wrong place." The brown leather shoes stepped to one side. "Dumb, stupid fool!"

The Jittery Man didn't say anything to defend himself.

I had to find a way to get the Jittery Man and the Greasy Man out of the room. But how? I couldn't just knock and ask them to leave.

I rolled down the hallway and looked in through the next doorway. The plunk-plunk of dripping water filled the room. In the far corner stood a tall, A-frame stepladder. Some cardboard boxes lined one wall. A few rusting tools and a few boards were strewn here and there. Two paint buckets with wire-loop handles stood in the middle of the room. As my eyes adjusted further to the dark, I noticed large drops of water dripping from the ceiling into the two cans–both were almost full.

I thought about *Underhand Sam*, a suspense novel Uncle Dane had published a couple of years ago. The book's hero, a guy named Sam, confused the bad guys in one scene by setting off a delayed explosion. There was no way I was going to try to blow anything up, but I didn't think I'd need to. A loud noise would probably work just as well. In the book, Sam used sand pouring out of a small hole in a burlap sack as a timer. There were no bags of sand, but there were two cans full of water.

Moving as quietly as I could, I rolled into the room, took off my skates, then took stock of the tools I could use. There were pliers, an electric circular saw, a socket wrench set, a crowbar, and an old screwdriver. I picked up the screwdriver. Its blade was covered with rust, but the tip was still pretty sharp.

I grabbed the stepladder and placed it in the middle of the room. One of the boards was long, thick, and still solid. I placed it on the floor alongside the ladder. I then moved the paint cans so that each one stood near each end of the board. The buckets' wire handles were so stiff with rust, they stood up without my having to hold them. I slipped the board under the paint cans' handles then picked it up in the middle. The buckets dangled from the ends like a couple of upside-down kids on a seesaw. I lifted the board up overhead and centered it on top of the stepladder. When I let go, I found that they were balanced.

While holding one of the buckets with my left hand, I took the screwdriver in my right and stabbed the bottom of it. The old paint can was soft from decay, so the blade sliced into the metal like a hot knife through warm butter. I pulled out the screwdriver. A steady stream of water poured through the hole.

The bucket with the hole in it would soon become much lighter than the bucket without a hole in it. Both buckets and the board would fall to the concrete floor. It would make quite a racket. When that happened, I'd have to be ready.

I hurried back up the hallway then flattened myself against the wall between the street door and the one behind which the Jittery Man and the Greasy Man were going through Ms. Nattie's purse. As I stood there wondering how much time it would take for the buckets and the board to fall, a loud crash issued from the second room. It was even louder than I thought it would be. I heard the Greasy Man say, "What was that?"

The Jittery Man said nothing.

The door next to which I stood jerked open. Flashlights glaring, the two men rushed down the hallway. I dashed into the room they'd occupied. There on the table was Ms. Nattie's purse and what I assumed to be all of its contents. The bottle of capsules lay on its side near the edge of the table. I didn't have time to gather up all of Ms. Nattie's things. I grabbed the medication bottle, dashed out into the hall, then crashed open the front door.

I ran down the sidewalk as fast as I could. I didn't dare look back to see if the Jittery Man and the Greasy Man were chasing me. When I reached the end of the block and turned the corner, I felt the rough concrete chewing away at my socks. I dashed down the next street and found a bank of payphones. The soles of my feet were already sore, but I knew I'd better put more distance between me and the bad guys before I stopped. Once I reached a place of safety, I would call Dr. Gao and read him the label on the medication bottle. I could only hope it wasn't too late for Ms. Nattie.

# Chapter Six

After I'd run more blocks than I could count, I figured I was out of danger. The holes in the soles of my socks were so large, I was practically barefooted. I pulled off my socks and pitched them into a sidewalk trash can.

At the end of the next block, I found another payphone. When I picked up the receiver, I realized that I didn't know what number to call. I had no way of knowing to which hospital they had taken Ms. Nattie. I doubted that Pow Wow and his folks would have gone back to the hotel. I didn't know the Gaos' mobile number, but I did know my own. I hoped Pow Wow would still have my phone with him.

He answered on the second ring. "Hello?"

"Pow Wow – it's me."

"Zeke! Are you all right?"

"I'm fine. Where are you?"

"At the hospital."

"How's Ms. Nattie?"

"No word yet. Dad's in with her now. Mom and I are still waiting for him to–" Pow Wow stopped speaking in mid-sentence.

"Zeke, are you alright?" Mrs. Gao had taken the phone from Pow Wow. There was concern in her voice, but I could also tell she was angry with me.

I tried my best to sound convincing. "I'm fine, Mrs. Gao."

"Where are you?"

I looked up at the street sign and told her the intersection at which I was standing.

"Do you have cab fare?"

I still had money in my pocket, so I said, "Yes, ma'am."

She gave me the name and address of the hospital then added, "Jump in a taxi and come right here."

"Mrs. Gao?"

I heard her take a deep breath. She was obviously trying not to lose her temper with me. "What is it, Zeke?"

"Do you have a pen and some paper?"

Her tone suddenly changed. "Yes. Why?"

"I got Mrs. Winthrop's medication bottle."

"Hold on." I heard some rummaging sounds, then Mrs. Gao came back on the phone. "Tell me everything on the label."

I read to her the name of patient – Mrs. Nattie Winthrop – the name of her doctor, the type of the medication, and its dosage.

When I started reciting the pharmacy and the prescription number – a string of nine digits – Mrs. Gao interrupted by saying, "Good work, Zeke. I'll get this information to the doctors." Mrs. Gao's tone changed from proud to annoyed again. "Now get yourself to the hospital right away, young man. No detours. We'll be in the emergency waiting room."

During the cab ride to the hospital, I thought about what had happened. Mrs. Winthrop's life may very well have depended on it, but I could have gotten hurt, if not worse. I started thinking about everything that could have gone wrong. I hadn't been brave. I'd been stupid. If things hadn't gone exactly right, the Jittery Man and the Greasy Man could have captured me. The Jittery Man knocked down an elderly lady, and the Greasy Man didn't even care if she'd gotten hurt. There was no telling what they might have done to me. I was so nervous, my hands started to perspire. As we rode along, I looked out at the city while keeping the bottle clasped tightly in the palm of my sweaty left hand.

When the taxi pulled up near the hospital's emergency room entrance, I fished out some folded-over bills and paid the driver. I stuffed the change back into my pocket and stepped out of the cab. As I made my way into the emergency room entrance, I thought again about the cabbie who'd helped me track down the Jittery Man. I would have to remember to track him down and repay him.

Pow Wow and his mom were standing in one corner of the ER waiting room. When Mrs. Gao saw me, she ran over and hugged me so hard it almost hurt. She then pulled away and said, "Young man, we were worried sick." The expression on her face could have been either a grimace or a smile. A door marked "No Admittance" flew open. Dr. Gao hobbled over to me on his crutches. I handed him the prescription bottle.

He took it and asked, "Where's the label?"

I looked at the bottle and realized that the label was missing.

"I– I– I…don't know." Then, I remembered my perspiring palms. "My hands were all sweaty. I guess the label fell off in the cab."

Dr. Gao shrugged. "It doesn't matter. Mrs. Winthrop's doctor is in with her now. She's still unconscious, but at least they know how to treat her now." Pow Wow's dad paused for a moment, then he said, "Thanks to you, Zeke." He looked me in the eye and said, "Do you know what you've done?"

I didn't know what to say, so I said nothing.

"The information you gave Jeannie over the phone may have very well saved Mrs. Winthrop's life."

For a moment, I wondered who "Jeannie" was. Then I realized that Dr. Gao was talking about his wife.

Pow Wow punched me on the arm and said, "Way to go, Sherlock!"

Dr. Gao bit his bottom lip for a moment then held up the label-less prescription bottle. "Should I even *ask* how you got this?"

I thought about it for a moment then replied, "You don't want to know." I paused a moment. "We need to call the police."

The Gaos looked at each other and nodded.

Dr. Gao said, "There's a detective in the emergency room. I'll go get him."

As he hurried away, Mrs. Gao looked down at my bare feet then handed me my sports bag. "You might want to put on some shoes."

# Chapter Seven

Dr. Gao went with us when the police detective took me into the small, empty hospital office to talk to me. Officer Paul Martino was about thirty-five years old. He had straight black hair and brown eyes. When he spoke, he sounded like a policeman in a gangster movie. He seemed like a nice man.

"You know, Zeke..." Detective Martino's voice tapered off. "If I had a son who did what you did, I'm not sure if I'd reward him or ground him." He smiled. "One thing's for sure, though, Nattie Winthrop is alive because of you."

I was starting to become self-conscious about all the attention. Even though it was better than having people yell at me, I still wished everyone would stop talking about it.

Detective Martino pulled out a notebook and said, "Now, suppose you tell me how you came to get Mrs. Winthrop's medication."

He took careful notes as I told him the story of how I had followed the Jittery Man to the building with the boarded-over windows then created a diversion so that I could grab the medication bottle.

"What about the label?"

I felt my face turn red. "I got pretty nervous after it was all over. My hands were really sweaty. I guess the label loosened up in my hand and fell off in the taxi."

Detective Martino didn't look angry, but he shook his head. "It'll take days to find the right cab."

"No, it won't."

He looked at me.

I recited the number stenciled on the cab's rear door.

He stared at me a moment.

Dr. Gao, speaking for the first time, said, "He has strong retention of numerical information."

Detective Martino said, "Could you repeat that?"

I rattled off the number again.

As Detective Martino closed his notebook, he said, "You'll probably be in for a big reward, Zeke."

"Reward?"

"Do you know whose life it was you saved?"

I nodded. "Nattie Winthrop."

"Yes, but do you know *who* Mrs. Winthrop is?"

I shook my head.

"She's the widow of Walter Winthrop – the real estate baron. Nattie Winthrop is one of the wealthiest people in New York City. Actually, she's one of the richest women in the world."

*Well,* that *explains the wad of money she pulled from her purse*. I muttered, "I thought she was poor."

"Why would you think that, Zeke?"

"When Pow Wow… I mean, when *Richard* and I met her at the concession stand, she was wearing this really old dress, and… I don't know. She just didn't seem rich."

Detective Martino smiled. "Word is, she's a bit eccentric. Won't throw out old clothes. Uses the same tea bag twice. Doesn't trust banks. You know the type."

I didn't really know the type at all, but I nodded anyway because I thought it was expected of me.

Dr. Gao and I got into an unmarked police car with Detective Martino. I sat up front. Dr. Gao got in the back seat with his crutches. Even though I hadn't noticed the name of the street on which the building with the boarded-over windows was situated, I thought I could find it if we started at the beginning.

I asked Detective Martino to drive to the Sherry-Netherland Hotel. From there, it took several minutes of winding through streets before we found the right building. Detective Martino then parked at the end of the block and called for backup.

While we waited, I told Paul Martino everything I could remember about the Jittery Man and the Greasy Man. When I said that the Greasy Man had done all the talking, Detective Martino seemed to find that interesting. He asked me in a couple of different ways if it was possible that I was mistaken. He was just doing his job, I knew, but it still bothered me a little that he questioned what Uncle Dane called my "powers of observation."

Several minutes later, another unmarked police car arrived at the scene. Detective Martino told Dr. Gao and me to stay in the cruiser with the doors locked. He then stepped out of the car and joined the two other plainclothes policemen. They walked down the street, opened the door of the boarded-over building, and walked inside. Just like that.

I looked at Pow Wow's dad and said, "I've got a funny feeling about this."

"About what, Zeke?" Dr. Gao glanced at the building.

"About what they're going to find in there."

Dr. Gao pushed his glasses up the bridge of his nose and said, "Why's that, Zeke?"

"Instinct."

Dr. Gao half-chuckled. Then, he looked at my face and saw that I was serious, so he quickly stifled the laugh.

A few minutes later, the police exited the building.

When Detective Martino approached the car, I unlocked the driver's side door.

He slid behind the steering wheel and said, "Son, are you sure this is the place?"

I nodded.

Detective Martino looked at Dr. Gao. "Okay if he comes with me?"

"As long as I can come, too."

With Dr. Gao on crutches, the three of us approached the boarded-over building and went inside. One of the plainclothesmen from the other car was holding a flashlight in the front room, the one in which the two men had been going through the contents of Mrs. Winthrop's purse. At least, I *thought* it was the same room.

The expensive-looking round table was gone. The room was empty. I quickly rushed out of that room and into the next. Detective Martino was right behind me. He shone his flashlight inside. The ladder, the buckets, the water, my inline skates – all were gone.

"Are you *sure* this is the right place?" It was Detective Martino.

I nodded. It made no sense. I was sure of what I'd seen. "I know this is the right place. I got Mrs. Winthrop's pills off the table."

"The table that doesn't seem to be there?"

I hung my head.

Detective Martino patted my shoulder. "Son, I know you're telling the truth about what happened. But this place isn't matching up with your description. And it seems a bit far-fetched that a purse-snatcher would go through all the trouble to empty the scene. Maybe you were in a building like this on another street?"

As Dr. Gao and I walked back to the unmarked police car, I mumbled "It *is* the right place."

Dr. Gao said, "I believe you, Zeke."

# Chapter Eight

Dr. Gao and I found Pow Wow and his mom sitting at a large square table in the middle of the hospital dining room. Mrs. Gao had a strange look on her face. "Mrs. Winthrop's stable but still unconscious. Dr. Long–" She looked at me and said, "Dr. Long is Mrs. Winthrop's personal physician. He's going to stay with her until they can contact a family member or a friend."

Dr. Gao thought for a moment before saying, "Does he have our mobile number?"

Mrs. Gao nodded, then asked, "How'd it go with the police?"

Instead of answering, Dr. Gao hobbled over to the buffet line and introduced himself to a tall, athletic-looking man wearing surgical scrubs and running shoes. Heart surgeon, I guessed. Dr. Gao spoke to the man for a while, then he hobbled back to where we sat. With a smile, he said, "Let's go for a ride."

I squeezed into a cab with the Gaos. Pow Wow's dad sat up front. He gave the driver an address. The taxi took off like a shot.

Back in Dallas, Mrs. Gao drove like she was competing in the Indianapolis 500. Our cabbie made her look like a real slow-poke. As the taxi careened through the streets of New York, I wondered where we were going, and if we would get there without having a wreck.

As we came to a sudden stop in traffic, Pow Wow asked once more what had happened with the police. Dr. Gao turned around gave his son a stare that stopped him from asking again.

Mrs. Gao cleared her throat then said, "Up ahead on the right, we have the Chrysler Building."

I looked out the window and saw the tall, gleaming structure. It looked like a big silver rocket ship, a rocket ship decorated with gargoyles. It was one of my favorite buildings. Mom said it was one of the structures that led her to study architecture.

Mrs. Gao continued, "Built in the Art Deco style, the Chrysler Building stands over 1,000 feet tall. When its spire was raised in 1929, it became the world's tallest structure, taller than even the Eiffel Tower in Paris. Its record would not last long, though. The Empire State Building was completed a few months later."

Mrs. Gao told us about Grand Central Station and, as we turned to head south on Fifth Avenue, she read the section of the book on the New York Public Library. We came to a stop in traffic in front of the library's main steps. Mrs. Gao pointed out the window and said, "They have names, you know."

Pow Wow's face screwed up into a question mark. "Who are you talking about, Mom?"

Mrs. Gao said, "The lions."

I glanced out the window to see the two enormous, pink-marble lions that lay on pedestals at either side of the stairs leading up to the library's entrance. I had never noticed them before. I looked at Mrs. Gao and said, "Do you know their names?"

She nodded. "Patience and Fortitude. We could all do with a little more of both."

Pow Wow took the copy of *New York Now!* from her hands and scanned the section on the library. "There's nothing in here about the lions." He looked at his mom, "Are you making that up?"

Mrs. Gao shook her head. She seemed very satisfied with herself.

Pow Wow looked at her and said, "How'd you know that?"

Dr. Gao turned to look back at us again. "How *did* you know that?"

Mrs. Gao just smiled.

Me, I still wondered where we were going.

# Chapter Nine

The taxi stopped in front of a two-story sports store full of high-dollar merchandise. I couldn't figure out what was going on. After we stepped out onto the sidewalk, I elbowed Pow Wow and asked, "Why are we here?"

He shrugged.

As the cab pulled away, Dr. Gao smiled and said, "Zeke, I think you'd find it hard to compete in the Big Apple Inline Skate-Off in your tennis shoes."

The store's "Foot-Mounted Wheels" department was huge. I'd never seen so many different types and brands of inline skates. The sales clerk was a young blond guy who looked like a surfer. He had a tattoo of a skateboard on his left forearm. Dr. Gao asked him if he could recommend an inline skate for racing. The clerk immediately pulled down the same model Pow Wow wore. I knew how much they cost, I knew how long Pow Wow had saved up to buy his, so I pointed out the display of an inexpensive model, gave the clerk my size, and told him some like that would be fine. Dr. Gao asked the clerk to bring out a pair of the ones Pow Wow wore.

The clerk listened to Dr. Gao. He brought out the model of skates Pow Wow wore. I put them on. They fit perfectly. I skated up and down the paved path that ran through the store. It was like floating on air. I loved those skates. Even so, they were too expensive. I took them off, handed them to the clerk, and said no thanks.

Dr. Gao said, "We'll take them."

While we were there, I got a new helmet to replace the one I'd ditched in the park. This time, I picked black, which I considered much better for sneaking around than bright-yellow one I'd lost. Pow Wow wasn't completely left out. He got a new skateboard. He'd always wanted one. He seemed happy with it, and I felt less guilty. As we left the store, I thanked Dr. Gao and told him that I would ask

Uncle Dane to pay him back when he arrived in New York.

Dr. Gao replied, "We'll discuss it later," then he hobbled on ahead to hail a cab.

As we walked back out onto the noisy city sidewalk, Pow Wow smiled. "When Dad says, 'We'll discuss it later,' that usually means 'We'll never discuss it again.'"

We went back to the hotel to get ready for dinner. Mrs. Gao asked us to put on the sport coats and ties we'd brought along. I felt like making a sour face, but I thought it would be rude, so I just said okay. That didn't stop Pow Wow from frowning. Mrs. Gao didn't seem to care. She just turned and headed down the hall toward their room.

Dr. Gao stayed behind to talk to us. He explained the concept of the trade-off: Pow Wow and I got to compete in the Big Apple Inline Skate-Off. Dr. Gao got to go to his conference. All Mrs. Gao asked in return was to be taken to nice places for dinner. Pow Wow and I agreed that that was reasonable.

"Too bad we couldn't get reservations at Tavern on the Green. That would have made the whole trip for her. Oh, well. Maybe next time." As Dr. Gao walked away, he said, "As for tonight, fellows, trust me – the food will be worth it."

While Pow Wow showered and changed clothes, I tried on my new inline skates. I knew I'd be able to go faster in them on the road, at least. In the room, though, I only managed to bump into the furniture. I took them off and placed them alongside Pow Wow's in the corner.

Pow Wow went into the hall to try out his new skateboard while I got cleaned up. When I came out of the bathroom, I was surprised to find him sitting on his bed. After a lot of quizzing, I found out that a pretty blonde lady on her way to the elevator had told him he looked adorable riding his skateboard in a coat and tie. Pow Wow didn't like being called "adorable."

We met Pow Wow's parents in the lobby. Dr. Gao looked a little funny in his dark suit walking on his crutches. Mrs. Gao was wearing makeup and a nice dress. She carried a small purse covered with sparkles. Her hair was even done up. She looked pretty. I knew I'd never hear the end of it from Pow Wow if I told her, so I just smiled.

As we stepped into yet another taxi, Mrs. Gao asked the driver to take us to the hospital. Dr. Gao knew how much the dinner meant to his wife, so he mentioned that we might lose our reservations if we were late. She said Mrs. Winthrop was more important than a nice dinner.

When we reached the hospital, we found out that they had moved Mrs. Winthrop to a private room. Dr. and Mrs. Gao seemed surprised by that. Pow Wow and I stayed in the lobby while his parents went to check on Mrs. Winthrop. They came back a few minutes later. Both had smiles on their faces.

Pow Wow's mom almost laughed when she said, "Mrs. Winthrop's awake!"

Dr. Gao added, "She'd heard all about the two young men who helped her. She wants to see you both."

Pow Wow and I rode the elevator to the seventh floor with his parents. When the doors opened, we walked out into the hall and saw a police officer standing guard by one of the doors.

The officer nodded at Dr. Gao, and the four of us stepped inside. I'd been in a lot of hospital rooms in my time, but I had never seen anything like that. It felt like I'd walked into a suite in really nice hotel.

Nattie Winthrop lay propped up in bed. Her silver-blue hair was mussed, and she had a large bandage on her forehead. A piece of white tape held the bridge of her horn-rim glasses together. She looked over at us, smiled, and, with her hand, made a weak gesture for us to come closer.

Before we could take a single step, a well-dressed man of about Mrs. Winthrop's age walked out of the bathroom holding a glass of water. He had slicked-back hair that looked to have been dyed black. A pink handkerchief was sticking out of the pocket of his dark suit coat. Even without being close enough to smell him, I knew he was wearing too much cologne.

The man looked at us and said, "I'm Xavier Dupont, an old friend of Natalie." His accent was French. "Please forgive my being impolite, but I've only just arrived. Who would you be?"

If my mom had been there, she would have called his tone arrogant. My dad would have just said he was full of himself. Uncle Dane would have told them both not to make snap judgments.

Dr. Gao hobbled over to shake the man's hand. "I'm Steve Gao." He waved one of his crutches toward where Mrs. Gao, Pow Wow, and I were standing by the door. "Monsieur Dupont, this is my wife, Jeannie, our son, Richard, and our friend, Zeke Armstrong." Dr. Gao chuckled and said, "You can probably figure out which one of the boys is which."

Pow Wow and I laughed. Monsieur Dupont just stood there. He didn't even smile.

Mrs. Winthrop's voice was weak but determined. "Xavier, these young men saved my life. Richard called the ambulance, then he and his father rode with me to the hospital. It was Zeke who recovered my bottle of capsules, which allowed the doctors to treat me for my ..." She held one hand lightly to her chest and cleared her throat. "Little condition."

Monsieur Dupont made an odd gesture toward us. The gold watch on his wrist sparkled as he moved his arm. "Thank you, boys. Thank you for helping Natalie."

Mrs. Winthrop looked up at Monsieur Dupont and said, "Xavier is a dear, old friend whom I've only recently rediscovered. We met in high school. He was a foreign exchange student from Lyon. He lived with the family next door. What a magical year that was." She smiled at us again. "After Xavier returned to France, we fell out of touch. A few weeks ago – the day after my son and his family left for India, in fact – I was walking down the sidewalk feeling quite alone in the city. Just when I was at my lowest point, I ran into Xavier on the sidewalk." Mrs. Winthrop looked up at Monsieur Dupont. "Such a coincidence."

Pow Wow's mom whispered, "I'll bet," under her breath. It sounded like she was using what Uncle Dane called "sarcasm" – saying one thing but meaning the opposite. I agreed with Mrs. Gao. There was something wierd about Xavier Dupont. I was just glad we were standing too far away from the bed for him and Mrs. Winthrop to hear what Pow Wow's mom said.

"The days I spent in New York with Natalie were the happiest of my life. I've wanted to return here ever since I was an exchange student." Monsieur Dupont patted Mrs. Winthrop on the hand and said, "My dear wife died several years ago. We had no children. I never remarried. There was nothing tying me to France. Nothing except my businesses, of course. Now that I have sold them, I am retiring here in New York City. Natalie and I have all the time in the world to catch up."

Mrs. Winthrop closed her eyes for a moment. It was obvious that she was tired. Dr. Gao glanced at his watch and said we had to be going or we would miss our reservations. Mrs. Winthrop asked if we would stop by the following morning. Pow Wow's mom said we would.

Before we left, Monsieur Dupont walked over and shook hands with Pow Wow and me. Pow Wow had a big smile on his face. I had to try my best not to frown. When Xavier Dupont bent over to kiss the back of Mrs. Gao's hand, she made a face like she'd just bitten into a lemon.

As Xavier Dupont turned to walk back to Mrs. Winthrop's bedside, I noticed his shoes. They were well-polished and expensive-looking, but the soles were worn thin. I wondered if he, too, was weird about money, like Mrs. Winthrop.

# Chapter Ten

In the taxi on the way to the restaurant, Mrs. Gao pointed out the window and said, "Look, boys, the Empire State Building!" She pulled her copy of *New York Now!* from the little sparkly purse she carried. I wondered how she'd fit it in there. She began reading. "From its completion in 1931 until 1973 – a span of over forty years – the Empire State Building was the tallest building in the world. It stands at a colossal 1,454 feet in height. Construction of the building was accomplished in only eighteen months, and it was done far under budget. The lobby features…"

As Mrs. Gao told us more about the Empire State Building than any of us probably wanted to know, I started thinking about seeing my parents again. Tomorrow couldn't come soon enough. By then, they would know whether or not Health for the World would have the funding they needed to continue their work.

After passing a few more buildings and getting more travelogue from Mrs. Gao, we reached Manhattan's Little Italy. Arrivederci was a *nuovo italiano* restaurant on Mulberry Street that Mrs. Gao had read about in *The New York Times*. When the maitre d' seated us at our table, I saw three forks on one side of my plate, and two spoons on the other. Pow Wow elbowed me and said, "Which one do we use for what?"

I shrugged and said, "Start at the outside and work your way in."

Mrs. Gao smiled and nodded.

The waiter brought plates filled with food I'd never seen before – and I've seen a lot of things. In my thirteen years, I'd lived in seven foreign countries and visited several others. In many of those places, my parents and I would eat with the natives. Sometimes, for the sake of being good guests, we had to eat things most people would be squeamish about stepping on. Once, in New Guinea, we actually ate beetles. Live beetles. They weren't as bad as you might think they would be.

Whatever the food at Arrivederci was, it tasted great. When dessert came and we got to use our second spoon, Mrs. Gao cleared her throat and said, "So, what did you guys think of Monsieur Dupont?"

While Pow Wow was saying, "I liked him a lot," and his dad was saying, "He seems like a good man, I said, "I didn't like him very much."

Pow Wow looked at me like he'd just found out I was from the planet Mars. "Why don't you like him?"

I shrugged. "There's something kind of slimy about him."

Pow Wow said, "How could you say that about such a nice old man?"

Mrs. Gao spoke so softly, we all had to strain to hear. "Just because he's an old man, Richard, it doesn't mean he's nice." She then took a bite of her dessert.

# Chapter Eleven

It was nighttime when we left Arrivederci. We went straight back to the hotel. Dr. Gao told us to get right off to bed so we'd be fresh for our race tomorrow. Pow Wow and I went to our room. While I was at the sink brushing my teeth, there was a knock at the door.

I walked out of the bathroom and spoke around my toothbrush. "Who is it?"

"I don't know." Pow Wow looked through the peephole.

"It's a bellhop. A lady bellhop. She's holding a big box tied up with a ribbon."

"Who'd be sending us a present?"

Pow Wow scrunched up his face for a moment, then he smiled. "Mrs. Winthrop! She probably sent us something for saving her life."

"You think so?"

He nodded.

When I went back to the sink to rinse out my mouth, I heard Pow Wow open the door.

He said, "Thank you." The door slammed shut a moment later.

As I dried my face, I yelled, "Don't open it without me!"

"Okay, but you better get in here!"

I walked out of the bathroom. Sitting in the middle of my bed was a dark-green box tied up with a bright-blue ribbon.

Pow Wow looked at me. "I wonder what it is."

"Me, too."

We looked at each other, then I said, "Well, since neither of us has X-ray vision, I guess there's only one way to find out." I grabbed one end of the ribbon while Pow Wow grabbed the other. We pulled. The bow came undone and the ribbon fell away. Pow Wow grabbed the lid with both hands and yanked it off.

Of all the things I'd expected to find inside, I never would have expected what I saw. Lying there, in the middle of the box, was a snake! It was a rattlesnake, a timber rattler as best I could tell. Its tail began to vibrate as it coiled up in strike position. The rattle made an eerie sound that sent chills up my spine. The snake flicked its forked tongue.

Pow Wow ran for the door. I did as I'd been told by the snake charmers I'd met while visiting my parents in India – I stood still. All at once, it occurred to me that Pow Wow was doing exactly what the person who delivered the package expected us to do.

"Stop!" I yelled over the buzzing of the snake's rattle.

Pow Wow froze in his tracks.

Something told me that going out into the hall would be a very bad idea. In a soft tone, I said, "I'm not sure why, but whoever sent this snake wants us out of this room." I paused a moment. "Deadbolt the door."

In the corner of my eye, I could see Pow Wow giving me another *Are you from Mars?* look. I said, "You can stay by the door if you want, but please deadbolt it."

Pow Wow did as I suggested.

In a low tone of voice, I asked, "What did the bellhop look like?"

Pow Wow asked, "Why?"

Keeping an eye on the timber rattler in the box, thinking about the tricks the snake charmers in India used, I picked up the lid with my right hand while I held up my left – well out of striking distance – and started waving it slowly back and forth. I only hoped the cobra trick would work on a rattlesnake. "It's important, Pow Wow. What'd she look like?"

"Really tall, skinny, long blond hair, a lot of makeup. I know it's not nice to say, but she was kind of ugly."

"Are you sure it was a woman?"

"Well, she was wearing a dress…"

I glanced back at him. "And…?"

Pow Wow glanced at the door. "What about her hair?"

"Could it have been a wig?"

He paused then nodded. "It could have."

"What'd she… *he* say to you?"

"Nothing. Not a word. He… She… The bellhop just handed me the box then walked away."

I remembered how the Jittery Man hadn't said anything when I found him in the boarded-over building with the Greasy Man. I wondered if the Jittery Man – disguised as a woman – had brought the snake to our room.

I remembered how the Jittery Man had stopped and looked back when Nattie Winthrop fell to the ground. The Greasy Man had chastised him for caring about her well being. The Jittery Man had not intended to harm her then. My gut was telling me he didn't want to hurt us now. I hoped my gut was right.

"This snake has probably been defanged." Still waving my left hand, I grasped the lid by the edges with the fingertips of my right hand, then carefully positioned it over the top of the box. "I don't want to take any chances, though."

I dropped the top. The snake half-struck at it as the lid fell onto the box. I grabbed the book I was reading from the nightstand beside my bed and used it to push the top on tight. The rattling from within stopped.

It took some doing, but I got Pow Wow to help me tie the ribbon back onto the box. We didn't bother making a fancy bow.

I said, "I think you should call your dad."

"You got it, Sherlock." Pow Wow headed for the phone on the nightstand. "Let me guess – you want him to call the police and bring hotel security with him."

"Brilliant deduction, Watson."

# Chapter Twelve

Dr. Gao and the hotel detective were at our door in less than three minutes. Two uniformed police officers arrived a short time later. They lifted the box's lid slightly then quickly shut it. One of them used the hotel phone to call and ask that a reptile specialist be brought in.

While we waited, Pow Wow gave the other officer a description of the bellhop who'd delivered the box. The officer asked the hotel detective if there were any female bellhops employed at the hotel. He shook his head and said, "Not at this time."

Pow Wow said, "I don't think it was really a woman. I think it was a man disguised as a woman."

Dr. Gao told the officer about the day's events, how I had recovered a stolen bottle of medication from a lady's purse. The officer asked if there was any way the "perpetrators" – he was talking about the Jittery Man and the Greasy Man – could have found out where I was staying. He shook his head. The officer told him it was probably a coincidence, but he decided it would probably be best to call in Detective Martino.

A pretty lady with dark-red hair and bright-green eyes reached our room a short while later. She was carrying a small, black box and a long orange stick-like thing with a claw on the end. She talked to the police officer at the door. He pointed at Pow Wow and me. She smiled as she introduced herself. "I'm Emily Mars. I'm the herpetologist."

I didn't know what a "herpetologist" was.

From the way Pow Wow looked at her, she must have guessed that he didn't know what the word meant, either. "Herpetologists study reptiles and amphibians. You know, snakes, frogs, and the like. I consult on cases with the New York City police department. I'm here because they asked me to take a look at the little present you guys received."

She walked over to the bed and dropped the box onto it. She held up the stick-like device, opened the claw at the end, and said, "Let's see what you've got."

Ms. Mars opened the box and, using the claw, grabbed the rattlesnake. It was about three feet long and squirming around. She grabbed it just behind the head with her hand. "Timber rattlesnake. Indigenous to New York State. Threatened species." When the snake opened its mouth, she said, "This specimen has been defanged."

I was right!

One of the policeman jotted something down in the notebook in which he'd written what Pow Wow told him about the bellhop.

Ms. Mars opened the black box, dropped the rattler inside, then shut and locked the lid. "There ya go, little fella. You'll be all nice and cozy in there."

Ms. Mars spoke to Dr. Gao. "Even if the snake had bitten your son or his friend, it could only have hurt them if they'd had a heart attack or if the wound had gotten infected." She looked at us for a moment. "Neither prospect seems likely. These guys look to be in tip-top shape." She held up the canvass bag. "And rattlesnakes have 'clean' bites."

Emily Mars looked at the police officer near the door. "I'm not trying to do your job, but I don't think this snake was sent to harm these guys. I think it was sent to scare them out of the room. There may be something in here they wanted."

The police officer nodded. "We'll call in the K-9 Unit."

Dr. Gao, Pow Wow, and I were taken down to the Gaos room. Two uniformed policemen stood guard at our door. Dr. and Mrs. Gao were incredibly calm, all things considered. I called Uncle Dane's mobile number, but hung up when I got his voice mail. This was the kind of news to be delivered in person, not by way of an electronic recording. I would tell him when he reached the city tomorrow.

Half an hour later, Detective Paul Martino knocked on our door. He said that a quantity of a "controlled substance" had been found in the room in which Pow Wow and I were staying. He mentioned that it seemed a pretty small quantity for such an elaborate measure, but he added that "criminal types" rarely made sense. He told the Gaos that Pow Wow and I weren't suspects, that the contraband had apparently been hidden in the room by a previous occupant. Mrs. Gao asked what the contraband was, but the detective didn't answer. He just said that, for our own safety, we would be moved to another hotel.

Dr. and Mrs. Gao packed quickly. Detective Martino and two other plainclothesmen carried their luggage as they took us down a service elevator. While we descended, Mrs. Gao asked about Pow Wow's and my belongings. One of the plainclothesmen told us that everything was being taken care of. When we reached the loading dock in back of the hotel, a burly Polynesian man with arms like tree trunks was piling Pow Wow's and my sports bags and our other luggage into the trunk of a big black Mercedes with tinted windows.

The burly man – he was also a police detective – drove us halfway across town then back through Central Park. He nosed the Mercedes down into an underground parking garage on the Upper West Side. There, along with our luggage, we were transferred to a big black van. After another trip through Central Park and a drive through countless city blocks, we pulled around to the back of a large hotel – a different hotel – and stopped at the loading dock.

An unmarked police car pulled in behind the van. Detective Martino got out of it and then escorted us through the back door of the new hotel. Inside, we were met by a neatly groomed, middle-aged man who introduced himself as Mr. James.

Mr. James and Detective Martino spoke in private for a moment, then they took us up a service elevator to the top floor. We walked down a short hallway and into an enormous room, larger than Uncle Dane's loft apartment in Dallas. Through a pair of French doors near one corner of the room I saw an enormous balcony ringed with large, potted trees.

Mr. James said, "The Imperial Suite." Like a flight attendant pointing out the exits during pre-takeoff, Mr. James motioned toward a door on the left side of the room. "King bed there." He nodded to the two doors to the right. "Queen bed there, and two full beds there." He walked a few steps forward then turned to face us. "Fully stocked kitchenette. Complimentary, round-the-clock room service. A private car and driver are standing by to take you wherever you wish to go." He crossed his arms. "An additional suite will be at your disposal when the rest of your party arrives."

It took me a moment to realize that "the rest of your party" meant my parents and Uncle Dane.

Mrs. Gao covered her mouth and said, "Oh, my."

Dr. Gao whistled and said, "What's this going to set us back?"

Detective Martino smiled and said, "Nothing."

Dr. Gao looked shocked. "Last I heard, the NYPD wasn't exactly rolling in dough."

Detective Martino laughed. "One look at my paycheck will tell you that."

Mr. James cleared his throat. "You've got friends in high places."

Dr. and Mrs. Gao, Pow Wow, and I exchanged confused looks.

Mr. James smiled. "Your accommodations are being provided by the hotel's owner. She wants you to enjoy the remainder of your time here in our fair city."

"Who's the hotel's owner?" As soon as I asked the question, though, I thought I knew the answer. "Mrs. Winthrop?"

Mr. James nodded. "I'm her assistant. She asked me to take good care of you." He looked at me and said, "Mr. Armstrong, I would like to extend to you my personal thanks for what you did. Mrs. Winthrop's a wonderful lady."

"But how did she know about…"

Detective Martino chuckled and said, "I hope you don't mind, but I made a couple of phone calls."

Mrs. Gao, who was still in shock, mumbled, "We don't mind a bit."

Mr. James walked to the door and said, "I'll have the hotel manager register you under an assumed name, just as a precaution."

I blurted out, "How about Ezekiel Tobias?" I looked at Dr. Gao. "It'll make it easier for my parents and Uncle Dane to find us."

Dr. Gao smiled and nodded.

Mr. James said, "Certainly. Mr. Tobias it is."

As the Gaos and I explored the suite, Detective Martino joined Mr. James near the door. I couldn't hear everything they said, but I knew they were talking about security measures. When I slipped around the corner to check out what sorts of goodies had been stocked in the kitchenette, I couldn't see Detective Martino and Mr. James, but I could hear them. They obviously didn't know I was standing there.

Detective Martino said, "Word on the street is that she has a bundle of cash and more gemstones than Tiffany's in a vault in her apartment. I hear she has another stash just like it in a secret location somewhere else in the city. She and her son are supposably the only ones with the combination, and, from what I hear, it's a really long string of numbers."

I thought it was funny the way Detective Martino said, "supposably" when he meant "supposedly."

Mr. James said, "I know not that of which you speak, Detective. Even if I did, I'm really not at liberty to discuss–"

"Ah, come on." Detective Martino chuckled. "I like the old girl. She's good people. I know she doesn't trust banks, and I hear the vaults are supposably pretty high-tech, but it seems awfully risky for her to keep that kind of loot lying around the house. Would you talk to her about it?"

Mr. James spoke softly. "Well, to be honest, I'm not sure if she'll listen. Ever since that French–" He paused. "For the past few weeks, Mrs. Winthrop hasn't been too keen on hearing what I think."

Detective Martino make a clicking sound with his tongue. "Well, her son will be back in a couple of days. Do you hold any sway with him?"

"A bit."

"Would you talk to him about it?"

Mr. James was silent.

When Detective Martino said, "Thanks," I figured Mr. James had nodded yes.

## Chapter Thirteen

As soon as Mr. James left, Mrs. Gao hurried about getting us settled in. Dr. Gao tried to help, but there wasn't much he could do hopping on one foot or hobbling around on crutches. Pow Wow and I offered to lend a hand, but Mrs. Gao said the best way we could help would be to get to bed.

Once we were in our room, Pow Wow stood beside the nightstand inspecting the lamp. He looked under the shade, then he ran his hand down along its electric cord.

"What are you doing?" I asked.

"Trying to find the switch."

I walked over and touched the lamp's metallic base. The light came on.

"How'd you do that?" he asked.

"Touch-sensitive switching. Uncle Dane has one of these in his office. Watch this."

I went into the bathroom, dampened a washcloth with warm water, then walked over to the nightstand. I touched the washcloth to the lamp's base. The light switched off. Pow Wow tried it a couple of times before he lost interest.

Long after Pow Wow had gone to sleep, I was still wide awake. I couldn't stop thinking about what happened. Everyone talked about what a strange coincidence it was, the snake package coming right after I'd snatched Nattie Winthrop's medication back from the bad guys.

If there was one thing I'd learned in my thirteen years of life, it was that coincidences did happen. Some twists of fate were downright eerie, but they were flukes just the same. Besides, I couldn't figure out any way that the Jittery Man or the Greasy Man could have known who I was, much less which hotel I was staying in. The only thing that made sense was the conclusion Detective Martino reached: The snake had been sent by the people who'd hidden the contraband in our room.

I got out of bed, walked over to the window, and pulled open the curtains. The lights of New York were spread out below like flecks of shiny silver and gold on a big black blanket. Uncle Dane called Manhattan "Shark City." I thought at first he meant that it would eat you up if you weren't careful, but he said I misunderstood. He loved New York. It was a city that never slept, so he thought of it as an enormous shark that had to keep moving to stay alive. When I mentioned that the Sleeping Sharks of the Yucatan in Mexico didn't have to swim all the time, he told me I was being difficult. A few moments later, he complimented me on finding a flaw in his logic. Even so, he continued to call it Shark City.

From now on, I might just call it Snake City.

No matter how little sense it made, a small part of me couldn't help but wonder if the snake in the box was connected to my recovering Nattie Winthrop's medication. If that were the case, though, why would they try to get Pow Wow and me out of our room? What could they have wanted? I'd given the bottle of capsules to Dr. Gao, who'd given it to the emergency room doctors. The bottle's label had fallen off in the taxi. Since I'd been able to give the police the cab's number, I figured they must have had the label by now. I had taken nothing physical away from the adventure. All I had were memories. Could the snake have been intended to scare me into forgetting?

When thoughts like that started going through my brain, I knew I must be really tired. With the big race tomorrow, I needed all the rest I could get, even if it was only a few hours' worth. I decided to go back to bed and try to get some sleep.

# Chapter Fourteen

I didn't sleep very well. I had dreams of snakes in boxes and playing hide-and-seek with the Jittery Man – whose face I saw as having no eyes and no mouth. Worst of all, though, I kept having a nightmare about a television reporter chasing me and asking if I were the real Ezekiel Tobias.

There was a very good reason for the nightmare. Uncle Dane had gone to California to talk to a producer interested in making a movie from *Ezekiel Tobias and the Deadly Darts*, the book that retold an adventure I'd had in Indonesia a few years ago. If that happened, it would be good for Uncle Dane, but it meant that more people would want to find out who Abraham Grey really was.

If that happened, it would only be a short time before my secret—that I was the real Ezekiel Tobias – would be out. It was bad enough, having Pow Wow and the other guys on our soccer team calling me Sherlock and things like that. I didn't think I could handle having everyone at school knowing the truth.

My mobile phone rang before the sun came up the next morning. It was Uncle Dane. He had bad news. Though he was supposed to have taken the red-eye, the plane was grounded for mechanical problems. He'd been rebooked on another flight this morning, but it would barely get him to the city in time for his interview with *The New York Times*. From there, he would go straight to the dinner Mrs. Gao had arranged at a French restaurant on the Upper East Side.

Things went from bad to worse. Uncle Dane had heard from my parents. Like the other members of Health for the World, Mom and Dad flew on special standby tickets when they traveled. This saved the organization a lot of money. The problem was, it sometimes took them a bit longer to get from place to place. That was the case today. Mom and Dad had gotten bumped from the Paris to New York flight, so they were having to fly from France to Miami, and from there take another plane to New York. They, too, would be meeting us at the restaurant.

No one in my family would be there to see me race. I was disappointed, of course, but I tried to look on the bright side. Dr. and Mrs. Gao would be there to see me cross the finish line. A few hours later, I would be with my family.

I tried to get back to sleep, but it was no use. Pow Wow had slept through my mobile phone ringing, as well as my conversation with Uncle Dane. He slept like everything that had happened to us in New York was completely normal. I didn't see how he could do that.

# Chapter Fifteen

When the alarm in my sports watch sounded, I was still awake. I got out of bed, went to the window, and looked out. The sky was blue, and the flags on the sides of the building were fluttering in the breeze. It was another beautiful day.

I walked out of our room. The French doors stood open. Pow Wow's parents were sitting in the middle of the balcony at a wrought-iron table. Dr. Gao was reading the newspaper. Mrs. Gao was working a crossword puzzle. There was enough food on the table to feed a small African village.

Mrs. Gao looked up at me and smiled. "Good morning, Zeke. Are you hungry?"

I was starving. I sat down at the table, drank a whole glass of fresh-squeezed orange juice, then I began to eat.

Halfway through my scrambled eggs, a voice behind said, "Hey, save some for me!"

Pow Wow and I tried to eat everything on the table. We had to stop, though, because we were afraid of getting sick during the race. There was still a lot left. After the bad conditions I'd seen in the countries in which I'd lived, I hated wasting food. I wondered if we should wrap it up and take it to one of the homeless people I'd sometimes see on the sidewalk.

I asked Mrs. Gao if we could do that. She said it was an excellent idea. I didn't really expect her to do anything about it. Parents will sometimes say something's a good idea, even though they don't intend to follow up on it.

Dr. Gao looked at his watch. "We have about an hour and a half before you guys need to start warming up. How about we go by the hospital, check on Mrs. Winthrop, and thank her for putting us up in such a nice place?"

Pow Wow and I nodded.

"Let's get going."

Pow Wow and I went into our room to get dressed. I couldn't find any clean shorts, so I put on the ones I'd worn the day before. Pow Wow and I quickly threw our inline skates and the rest of our gear into our sports bags. Back in the main room, I saw that Dr. Gao was wearing a big black backpack. It reminded me of the one the Jittery Man had worn. Dr. Gao said he wore it because it didn't get in the way of his crutches. Mrs. Gao was carrying a canvas bag large enough to hold fifty copies of *New York Now!*

When we walked out of the front of the hotel, a man in a chauffeur's suit and hat was waiting beside a large, black sedan. He asked if we were the Tobias party. The Gaos looked at each other. I said, "Yes."

Dr. Gao said he'd ride "shotgun," which meant in the front passenger seat. Pow Wow, Mrs. Gao and I sat in the back. As the chauffeur drove us to the hospital, we talked about how little traffic there was, and how few people there were on the sidewalks. As we turned down one street, I saw a ragged-looking woman sitting by a building and surrounded by some big, old shopping bags. I wished Mrs. Gao had wrapped up the food to give to her. No sooner had I thought that, Mrs. Gao said, "Stop the car!"

The driver pulled over to the curb. Mrs. Gao lowered the rear window and asked the woman if she was hungry. She nodded and came to the car. Mrs. Gao reached into the large canvas bag and passed her several plastic-wrapped packages. It was the leftover breakfast! The lady smiled. She was missing a couple of teeth in front. She said thank you and walked back to where her bags were lying on the sidewalk.

When the Gaos and I reached the hospital room, there was no uniformed policeman waiting outside in the hall. The door stood open. Nattie Winthrop's bed was unmade. An old leather suitcase sat atop it. Xavier Dupont was bent over rummaging through the bottom drawer of the nightstand.

Mrs. Gao cleared her throat.

"Oh!" Monsieur Dupont almost jumped off the ground as he stood up straight. He looked at us and said, "The Gao family, and young Zeke Armstrong. You surprised me."

Before I even thought about what I was doing, I said, "*Désolé, monsieur.*"

Pow Wow looked at me like I'd just sprouted antennae.

Xavier Dupont smiled and, in French-accented English, said, "Where did you learn French, young man?"

"*C'est ma langue maternelle.*"

Again in English, he said, "Where is your mother from?"

I gave up trying to speak French to him. "Paris." I didn't see any reason to tell him that she lived in France only six years, that her father was in the diplomatic service, that almost all of her life had been spent moving from one country to another.

Monsieur Dupont seemed on the verge of saying something else, but Mrs. Gao interrupted. "We came by to check on Mrs. Winthrop. Is she here?"

"She is… How do you say? Indisposed?"

Dr. Gao nodded.

"Me, I am preparing her immediate departure from this dreadful place." At that, Monsieur Dupont approached us. "I will of course tell her that you came here." He motioned us back through the door.

Monsieur Dupont was asking us to leave! I could hardly believe it. I wondered why he wanted us out of Nattie Winthrop's room. Pow Wow would probably say he was only trying to help her leave quickly. Me, I was annoyed. She'd asked us to come by.

As Xavier Dupont was closing the door, Nattie Winthrop exited the bathroom. "Oh, Zeke,

Richard! I was hoping you'd stop by. Please come in."

Monsieur Dupont pulled the door open and ushered us back inside. He acted like we'd just arrived. The expression on his face never changed.

Mrs. Winthrop still had the big white bandage on her forehead, but her hair was fixed and she no longer looked tired.

Mrs. Gao nudged Pow Wow.

He said, "Thank you for the suite, Mrs. Winthrop."

"Yes. Thank you," I added. "It's very nice."

She walked over to Pow Wow and me and wrapped an arm around each of us. "It's the least I can do. If not for you, I might not be here now."

As Dr. and Mrs. Gao started making conversation with Mrs. Winthrop, I noticed Monsieur Dupont standing by the bed. He wasn't smiling. In fact, he looked unhappy.

When Dr. Gao said that we needed to leave so Pow Wow and I could hydrate – his doctor word for "drink water" – Monsieur Dupont was suddenly in a better mood.

Mrs. Winthrop shook her head. "I won't hear of it. You've only just arrived." She turned to speak to Monsieur Dupont. "Xavier, would you be a dear and run down to the vending machine and get each of the boys a bottle of water?"

He smiled what appeared to me to be a forced smile. "But of course. It would be a pleasure." As he turned away from Mrs. Winthrop and walked out of the room, though, the smile disappeared.

After Mrs. Winthrop had chatted with the Gaos for a few moments, she turned her attention to me. "Tell me, young Mr. Armstrong, what did your parents think of your act of heroism?"

"They haven't heard about it yet."

She looked distressed.

"They're traveling. They're on their way here."

"From Dallas?"

"No, ma'am. India."

"India! My son and his family are on their way back from there now. They should be in New York tomorrow morning. They cut their trip short for me." She shook her head. "So sweet of them to worry about a silly old woman." Mrs. Winthrop looked at me. "I told you that my daughter-in-law is Indian, didn't I?"

I nodded.

"You didn't mention that your parents were visiting there."

"They're not visiting. They live there."

The conversation I'd been trying to avoid had started. I told Mrs. Winthrop what my parents did and how we had lived all around the world before I moved to Dallas. I mentioned that they might be coming to Dallas to live soon, since Health for the World's funding had decreased. Pow Wow's mom filled in the parts of my story that I'd left out, including how Abraham Grey was Uncle Dane's pen name, and how I was the Ezekiel Tobias in the *Ezekiel Tobias* books.

Mrs. Winthrop seemed very pleased at this. "My grandson, Nick, loves those books. What a treat it would be for him to meet you and your uncle. How much longer are you in the city?"

Mrs. Gao answered that we'd be there through the end of the week.

"Wonderful," is all Mrs. Winthrop said.

Dr. Gao looked at his watch and made his *We're going to be late* face.

Mrs. Winthrop was pretty sharp. She seemed to pick up on this right away. "Xavier isn't good with mechanical things. I'm afraid he may not be able to figure out how to work the vending machine. Either that, or he doesn't have enough change. He may need some help."

I volunteered. "I'll go."

Mrs. Gao seemed surprised by that – she didn't know that I was planning to do a bit of information gathering. She said, "Take Pow Wow with you. I want you guys to use the buddy system for the duration of our time in Manhattan." She smiled at Mrs. Winthrop. "No offense to your wonderful city."

"None taken, dear. You can never be too careful." She reached into her purse – a new purse – and handed Pow Wow and me some money. We started to protest, but she added, "No arguments."

We walked down the hall toward the vending machines at the end. As we drew near, I heard a man's voice. He was speaking in French.

I wondered if it was Monsieur Dupont.

With the announcements coming over the public address system, I couldn't make out everything the man said. I did hear enough to know that he was upset. He kept saying something about time running out.

Pow Wow and I reached the vending machines. I looked to my right and saw Monsieur Dupont sitting cross-legged on a chair in a little alcove. He was speaking on a mobile phone. The soles of his shoes – the same shoes he'd worn last night – were in bad need of repair. His watch flashed in the light. I doubted that it was real gold.

Monsieur Dupont looked our way, covered the mouthpiece of the phone and said, "Sorry, boys. I could not arrive at a solution for operating the vending machine. Then, I remembered an important telephone call that was necessary for me to make." He stood, reached into his pocket, retrieved some change and extended his hand toward us.

I said, "No thanks. We've got it covered."

Monsieur Dupont's expression never changed. "Very well. I will rejoin you shortly." He turned his back to us, sat, and continued talking, but no longer in French. It wasn't English, either.

He was speaking Wolof! I faced the vending machine and made the same sour-lemon face Mrs. Gao had made last night.

Pow Wow looked at me and mouthed the words, "Stop being mean!" He then fed some money into the slot.

I'd learned a few words and phrases of Wolof, the African tribal language, while my family and I were living in Senegal. I wondered how Monsieur Dupont had learned to speak it. For that matter, I wondered *why* he was speaking it now.

As the first bottle of water plunked down into the dispenser chute, I trained my ear to his conversation. Xavier Dupont kept using the words "*jot*" and "*juroom ñent*." I did a quick translation from Wolof to French, then from French to English. As best I could remember, "*jot*" meant "to get." "*Juroom ñent*" was "nine" – I was sure of that.

*Get nine*? Get nine *what*, I wondered.

As Pow Wow fed the money for the second bottle of water into the machine, I heard Monsieur Dupont say, "*Dañuy dem tej!*"

*We are leaving today.* That was an expression I knew well. Dad must have spoken that sentence a dozen times while we were in Dakar. He liked the city. It was just that he was ready to get back to work.

I wondered where Monsieur Dupont was going...and with whom. Since he didn't have any family and he was new to New York, I figured he must be taking Mrs. Winthrop on a trip. I wondered where they were going. For that matter, I wondered if Monsieur Dupont knew that Mrs. Winthrop's son and his family were on their way back from India.

Xavier Dupont then spoke a long sentence quickly. He repeated it a moment later, as if he were disagreeing with the person on the other end of the line. I could only understand four words. "*Jël*" meant take. "*Takkay*" was jewel. "*Xaalis*" was money. "*Roppëlaan*" meant airplane. The rest was gibberish to me. I wished I'd listened to my mom and paid more attention during our time in Dakar.

As best I could guess, Monsieur Dupont was planning to take Mrs. Winthrop on a plane trip – today. Why would he be taking money and jewels? Those would seem strange gifts, considering how wealthy Mrs. Winthrop was and how, according to

Detective Martino, she already had a lot of jewels in her safe.

The second bottle of water plunked down the chute. Pow Wow plucked it from the bin and said, "Let's go." I could tell he was really annoyed with me. He walked away down the hall without waiting for me. I wanted to listen to the rest of Monsieur Dupont's conversation, but that would look funny, me standing there by myself. I hurried to catch up with Pow Wow.

Halfway back to Nattie Winthrop's room, Pow Wow punched my shoulder and stopped. "What is it you don't like about Monsieur Dupont?"

"I think he's up to no good."

"Why do you think that?"

"Did you see the soles of his shoes?"

Pow Wow shook his head. "No. Why?"

"They were almost worn through."

"So what? He's probably just eccentric, like Mrs. Winthrop."

"I don't think so. It's like my Grandpa Lucky always says – you can tell a rich man from his shoes." My dad and my uncle's father, Tobias "Lucky Charm" Armstrong, had a lot of sayings. I guessed that's where Uncle Dane got his "pearls of wisdom."

Pow Wow just gave me another of those Martian looks.

That wasn't going to stop me from speaking my mind. "I think Monsieur Dupont is a phony. I think he's broke. I think he's out to marry Mrs. Winthrop so he can get her money."

Pow Wow started laughing. He laughed so hard, I wondered if he'd be able to breathe. When he finally got hold of himself, tears were running down his face. "That's the funniest thing I've heard in a long time." He laughed again. "I think you've been watching too many Alfred Hitchcock movies."

As we walked into Nattie Winthrop's room, Mrs. Gao blurted out, "Oh, my, you must have been frantic!"

I thought at first that they were talking about the Jittery Man stealing her purse, but then Mrs. Winthrop said, "Pete tried everything he could think of to get that door open. He even kicked it with his feet, but the lock was just too strong."

For a moment, I wondered who Pete was. Then, I remembered that he was Mrs. Winthrop's son.

Mrs. Gao turned to Pow Wow and me. "You boys stay away from abandoned refrigerators."

"Okay." I thought about it for a moment. "Why does everybody keep warning us about that?"

Dr. Gao's crutches clip-clopped as he came over to where we stood. "Mrs. Winthrop was just telling us about what happened when her son was a little boy. He was playing hide-and-seek with some of the kids in the neighborhood. He found one of those old-fashioned refrigerators – the kind with the latch on the outside – abandoned in an empty lot. He got inside, and the door locked. He couldn't get out. The kids he was playing with thought he'd gone home. He almost ran out of air. A policeman came by in the nick of time and heard Nick knocking." Dr. Gao looked down and smiled. "No pun intended."

Nobody laughed.

Mrs. Winthrop said, "I still have nightmares about it to this day. Whenever I build or buy anything, I think about what almost happened to my Pete."

The subject of conversation went from abandoned refrigerators, to New York architecture, and back to Mom and Dad's work in India. After a few minutes, Monsieur Dupont still hadn't returned to the room. Dr. Gao looked at his watch and said, "We need to get the boys to the park to warm up. Again, we thank you for your hospitality, Mrs. Winthrop."

"Nonsense. I haven't done nearly enough. Why don't you bring the boys by my apartment after the race this afternoon. I want to thank them properly."

Mrs. Gao said, "You've done too much already."

"Poppycock." She wrote out the address and passed it to Dr. Gao.

I looked around Dr. Gao's shoulder to see that Mrs. Winthrop's address was the same as it had been on the prescription label. She lived on Fifth Avenue, right next to Central Park. The cross-street she wrote on the paper was near where Pow Wow and I had made the wrong turn onto 72nd Street the day before. She lived in one of the most expensive places in the world, in a building with doormen and concierges. I thought again of how Pow Wow and I had believed her to be poor when she bought us the lemonades.

As Mrs. Gao was saying her good-byes, I remembered what Monsieur Dupont had said about leaving today. I wondered why Mrs. Winthrop would be inviting us to her apartment when she was going out of town. I asked, "When are you leaving?"

"In a few minutes."

That didn't make any sense. I guessed that she'd misunderstood me. "I meant, when are you leaving on your trip?"

"I'm not going anywhere, dear." She smiled. "Just home. Oh, Xavier's taking me by the pharmacy first. I have to pick up a new bottle of capsules."

# Chapter Sixteen

The hotel's big black car took us from the hospital to Central Park. The sun was shining, and the sky was blue. I was so distracted, I doubt I would have noticed if it had been raining. I wondered if I should mention to the Gaos what I'd heard Monsieur Dupont say about leaving today. Considering how Pow Wow had made fun of my theory, I decided to keep my mouth shut. Not only that, but my Wolof wasn't very good. I may have completely misunderstood what Xavier Dupont had said. It didn't really matter. We would see Mrs. Winthrop again in a few hours. There was no way Monsieur Dupont could marry her before then.

After Pow Wow and I checked in for the race, Dr. and Mrs. Gao decided to wait for us at the finish line. With all the walking on crutches Dr. Gao had done lately, his arms had gotten sore. He and his wife set up their folding chairs in a nice spot in the shade. I passed my mobile phone to them, then Pow Wow and I found a good patch of grass several yards away. We started pulling our gear from our sports bags.

Today, I was dressed all in black—black shirt, black socks, and the black shorts I'd worn yesterday. After strapping on my new black helmet, I pulled out my new black skates. The wheels should have been fresh and new, but they were worn. I didn't think I'd done that much damage to them just by skating around the store and in the hotel room. When I turned one of them over, I noticed a sticker from the airline we'd flown attached to the bottom of the boot. Pow Wow's real name and the name of our old hotel were printed on it in what I thought to be Mrs. Gao's handwriting. I flipped over the other skate. There was another label, printed with the same information.

I wasn't holding my skates. They were Pow Wow's. I glanced over to see my new skates sitting there in his open sports bag. We must have accidentally switched them while we were getting ready this morning. All at once, I realized that if Mrs. Gao put labels like that on the bottoms of Pow Wow's skates, she might have...

Chills went down my spine. I turned to Pow Wow and said, "I think I just figured out how the Jittery Man found us."

"What are you talking about, Zeke?"

"The snake at the hotel. It *was* the Jittery Man who brought it."

Pow Wow gave me another Martian look. "Zeke, there was contraband hidden in our room."

"Maybe *that* was the coincidence."

"Huh?"

"You heard what Detective Martino said. He thought it was a pretty small amount of...whatever it was for the guy in the disguise to have gone to such great lengths to get us out of that room."

Pow Wow didn't bother to look up from his helmet, which he was adjusting. "Right, Zeke."

I held up Pow Wow's skate, pointing the wheels at him, and said, "Did your mom put tags like these on the bottoms of my skates?"

He looked at it and said, "Guess we switched, huh?" He dropped his helmet then pulled one of the skates from his sports bag and flipped it over. There were no labels on the bottoms of my new skates.

"Not those," I said, "I'm talking about my old skates, the ones I left behind when I got Mrs. Winthrop's medication. Did she put those airline identification tags on them?"

Pow Wow shrugged. "Probably. She does that to my skis, to dad's golf clubs, to her tennis rackets. She has this thing about sports equipment getting lost in transit."

I nodded. "If she put my name and the hotel we were staying at on the bottoms of my old skates, then that could explain…"

"…how the Jittery Man found us?"

I nodded again. "The room you and I were staying in was registered to Uncle Dane – Dane Armstrong. He and I have the same last name."

From the way Pow Wow was looking at me, I could tell he was taking what I said seriously. He said, "Well, what do we do?"

"I think we should tell your parents."

Pow Wow thought about it a while, then he shook his head. "We don't even know if there were labels on the bottom of your skates."

"Yeah, but what if there were. If that's the case, we'll need to call Detective Martino."

"What if he doesn't believe you?"

"Why wouldn't he…" I realized that Dr. Gao must have told Pow Wow what happened when we went back to the boarded-over building. "He believed me about what happened. He just didn't think I'd found the right place."

Pow Wow nodded. "Okay, then. Tell me this: If the Jittery Man brought us the snake, why was he trying to get us out of our room?"

I didn't have an answer for that. "I don't know."

"I guess it doesn't matter. You're right – we should tell the police." Pow Wow frowned. "But let's wait until after the race."

"Why?"

"Because if my mom did put tags on the bottom of your skates – even if the snake had nothing to do with your getting back Mrs. Winthrop's medicine – she won't let us out of her sight for the rest of the trip." He shook his head. "Do you honestly think she'd let us race?"

## Chapter Seventeen

As Pow Wow and I made our way toward the staging area, something kept jangling in my pocket. It was the change from when I took the taxi to the hospital yesterday. I couldn't stand to have the coins banging around in there while I raced. I decided to tuck them into the elastic tops of my socks.

When I emptied my pocket, I found the coins, a few dollar bills...and something else. It was a wadded up piece of plastic-coated white paper. I smoothed out the wrinkles to see that it was a label—a prescription label.

"What's that, Zeke?"

I looked at Pow Wow. "The label from Mrs. Winthrop's bottle of capsules."

"I thought it had fallen off in the taxi."

"So did I. I must have accidentally stuffed it in my pocket with my change after I paid the cab fare." I stared at the label. There was the Mrs. Winthrop's address, the name of her doctor, the type of medication, the dosage, the long prescription number… All at once, it dawned on me. This could be what the Jittery Man was looking for.

"Oh, no." Pow Wow stopped as he made the same realization. "Do you think the Jittery Man wanted that label? Do you think that's why he sent us the snake?"

Hearing it said out loud, it seemed to make less sense. I shook my head. "It doesn't add up. Why would someone go to so much trouble just to get this little piece of paper?"

"Maybe there's something on it he wanted."

I looked at the information again. "Do you think he wanted her address?"

"Wouldn't that be on her driver's license?"

"I guess so." It all seemed so ridiculous. I put my hands on top of my helmet. "Maybe the label has nothing to do with anything. Maybe whoever hid the contraband in our room sent us the snake. Maybe the Jittery Man and the Greasy Man are long gone by now."

Pow Wow said, "Maybe…"

I took a long breath and let it out quickly. "I still think we should tell your folks."

"After the race, Zeke." Pow Wow seemed determined to participate in the Big Apple Inline Skate-Off. "As long as we stick together, we'll be safe."

I agreed – reluctantly – then tucked the label back into my pocket. Pow Wow and I took our place in the staging area on Park Drive for our age group. We decided that if we were going to race, instead of going directly to Pow Wow's folks to tell them about the label, we were going to race to win.

# Chapter Eighteen

The starting gun sounded. Pow Wow and I attacked right away. We quickly pulled ahead of the pack and took the lead.

Pow Wow was skating strong today. He seemed to have regained the stride he'd had before he came down with the flu. That good night's sleep he'd gotten last night had obviously helped.

We stayed side-by-side until we'd put what felt like a comfortable distance between ourselves and our nearest competition, a pack of five skaters. At that point, we agreed that I'd be the pull for the first half of the race. After that, I'd draft behind Pow Wow until we reached the final downhill. From that point to the finish line, it would be every man for himself.

We were skating hard, but we paced ourselves for the miles of race that lay ahead. As we passed 72$^{nd}$ Street, I thought of the wrong turn we'd made there yesterday. Today, there were officials on both side of the race path making sure we all stayed on course.

My new skates were amazing. They were so smooth, so fast. It felt like I was flying three inches above the road. The wind whistled through my new helmet at a different pitch than it had with my old helmet. My wheels sang the way Pow Wow's did.

There we were, in the lead. I knew I should have been concentrating on my stride and the race. Even so, I couldn't help but think about the label I'd found in my pocket. There was something about it that kept bugging me. My mind's eye kept focusing on the prescription number. There was something about it that made me think of Xavier Dupont.

I was so lost in my thoughts that, as we skated down a stretch of road between Cleopatra's Needle and the Metropolitan Museum, I barely noticed that the five guys who'd been behind us were passing us.

Pow Wow called out, "You want me to pull, Zeke?"

I glanced back and shook my head. "You keep drafting. We'll let 'em lead for now. We'll break out in the last quarter."

Getting my head back into the race, I focused the five-man break and paced myself to follow them, closely. Pow Wow wanted to win this race more than I did. I couldn't let him down. I owed it to him to help him do so. Either that, or win the race myself.

As we flew up the section of Park Drive squeezed between The Reservoir and Fifth Avenue, I looked through a gap in the wall and caught a glimpse of an armored car, one of those big trucks that picks up money from stores and delivers it to banks. It distracted me to the point that I almost broke my rhythm, but I tried to put it out of my mind. Pow Wow and I had a race to win.

Keeping my strokes as long and even as possible, we trailed the five-man break ahead by less than five yards – striking distance. Pow Wow's legs weren't as long as mine, but he was a stronger skater. I knew he could match my strides. We soon began passing some of the slower skaters who'd started in the heat previous to ours.

I should have stayed focused on winning. Even so, thoughts of Mrs. Winthrop, the prescription label, the armored car, and Monsieur Dupont talking on the payphone in the hospital filled my mind.

Next thing I knew, Pow Wow was skating alongside me. "Why'd you slow down, Zeke. Are you okay?"

I shook my head. "Something's wrong."

"Are you injured?"

"No. Nothing's wrong with me." I looked ahead and saw that the five-man break was pulling ahead. "I just keep getting this funny feeling. There's something about that prescription label, something important, something I'm missing. I can't shake the feeling that Mrs. Winthrop is in danger."

I expected Pow Wow to give me another one of those *Are you from Mars?* looks. Instead, he said, "You have good instincts about things like that. Do you want to go back and tell my folks now?"

"No. We've almost reached the halfway point." I glanced back and saw all the inline skaters behind us. "Besides, if we turn around now, we'll be like a couple of salmon swimming upstream."

"So what do we do?"

I shook my head. "I feel like I have important information locked up inside my head, but I don't have the combination to open the door."

Whatever it was Pow Wow said to me then, I didn't hear it. I reached into my pocket and pulled out the prescription label. Doing my best to watch where I was going, I looked at the prescription number:

782051263

It was nine digits long.

# Chapter Nineteen

Detective Martino had talked about the tremendous amounts of cash and jewels Mrs. Winthrop kept in her safe. In the safe to which only she and her son held the combination. It was a very long combination.

Mrs. Winthrop was bad with time, and she couldn't remember numbers. She would have picked a combination that she could find easily, something written on something she'd always carry. Since she had to take her medication every eight hours, she probably always carried her bottle of capsules. If the prescription number *was* the combination, it was one she would always have with her.

When Xavier Dupont was speaking on the phone in Wolof, I'd heard him say that he wanted nine of something. Could it have been nine numerals? A nine-digit combination?

All this time, I'd thought Xavier Dupont was out to marry Mrs. Winthrop for her money. I'd never considered the possibility that he might just try to *steal* it from her outright. He probably knew that Mrs. Winthrop always had the combination with her. It would make sense for him to put the Jittery Man up to stealing Mrs. Winthrop's purse to see if they could find the combination.

I went back to Xavier Dupont's conversation in Wolof. When he said, "We're leaving today," he wasn't including Mrs. Winthrop. He meant himself, the Jittery Man, and the Greasy Man. They were getting on a plane and taking...

Nattie Winthrop's money and her jewels!

I looked ahead and saw that we had fallen back to about ten yards behind the five-man break. Pow Wow was skating alongside me. I could tell from his face that he was concerned.

"Monsieur Dupont is after Mrs. Winthrop's money, but not the way I thought. He's trying to steal it from her."

Pow Wow kept skating. He didn't look at me like I was a Martian. He didn't call me Sherlock. He didn't say I was watching too many Hitchcock movies. He just said, "How?"

"He's going to rob her safe, maybe both of them. I think the prescription number is the combination. That's why he had the Jittery Man steal her purse. That's why he brought us the snake – so he could get us out of the room and look for the label."

"The Jittery Man and the Greasy Man…" Pow Wow's words trailed off.

I nodded. "They work for Monsieur Dupont. I'm sure of it. I'm also sure of something else – Mrs. Winthrop is in danger."

Pow Wow seemed deep in thought for a moment. "But if you've got the combination, won't she be safe?"

"Don't you remember what Mrs. Winthrop said? Monsieur Dupont was taking her by the pharmacy to get a new bottle of capsules."

"And it'll have–"

"The same prescription number on it. There's no telling what he might do to her after her gets that label."

Something had to be done. Right away. The Gaos had my mobile phone, so I couldn't call the police. Nattie Winthrop's apartment was less than thirty blocks from where we were. With a clear sidewalk and my fast inline skates, I could be there in a matter of minutes. It would be faster to skate there than it would be to try to find a phone.

"Pow Wow. I want you to skate faster than you've ever skated before. Finish the race, find your folks, and have them call Detective Martino. Send him over to Mrs. Winthrop's place right away."

Pow Wow nodded. "What are you going to do?"

"I'm going to Mrs. Winthrop's building."

He shook his head. "Zeke, I don't think that's such a good–"

"I'm not going up to her apartment. I'm just going to tell the doorman so he can call the police."

Pow Wow just looked at me.

"Don't worry. I'll be fine. I'm just going to warn her."

Pow Wow frowned.

102nd Street was just ahead. It was now or never. I passed him the prescription label and said, "Pour it on, Pow Wow. I've got to go."

"Don't do anything stupid."

As I peeled away from him, I yelled, "I won't!"

My wheels squealed as I made a high-speed turn off of Park Drive. I almost lost control as I came out of the cornering maneuver. After a short hop over to Fifth Avenue, I headed south and raced down the long stretch of sidewalk that ran alongside Central Park. I only hoped I wouldn't be too late.

# Chapter Twenty

Minutes later, I was across Fifth Avenue from Mrs. Winthrop's building. Parked in front of the building was a black Rolls Royce with darkly tinted windows. Its rear door was aligned with the maroon awning that stretched from the street to the front of the building.

The traffic on Fifth was light, but it was moving fast. Instead of risking being hit by a car, I skated to the crosswalk. Just as I reached it, the signal changed to walk.

Halfway across, I looked to my left to see the black Rolls Royce heading toward me. Just when I thought it should be slowing down, it began to accelerate. It was going to run the red light. If I didn't get out of the way, it was going to hit me!

I powered my way across the street. As I jumped the curb onto the sidewalk, air whooshed behind me. I did a fast T-stop to avoid running into a dark-blue baby carriage with big white wheels. I looked to my right and saw the Rolls racing away down Fifth Avenue.

The pretty dark-haired lady pushing the carriage asked, "Are you alright?"

"I'm okay."

"They ought to take away that old coot's license." The lady had a Southern accent. She looked like she had been born and raised on the Upper East Side. It sounded like she was from Mississippi. She pushed the carriage around the corner and headed down the side street.

I didn't have time to worry about bad drivers. I dashed up the sidewalk, then rolled under the awning in front of Mrs. Winthrop's building. There was no doorman out front.

I skated into the lobby. It was huge, like the inside of a cathedral. I called out, "Hello?" My voice echoed from the mahogany walls and the black-and-white marble floor.

No one answered.

I went to the concierge's desk. There was no one behind it. I rang the little brass bell that sat there on the counter. No one replied. I started getting another funny feeling in the pit of my stomach.

Something was wrong.

The first thing that occurred to me then was to go up to Mrs. Winthrop's apartment, but I knew that would have been a foolish thing to do. Instead, I rolled around to the back of the desk and removed my helmet. I sat it on the counter, then picked up the phone to call the police. The line was dead.

Something was very wrong.

Staying inside the building seemed a bad idea. Outside would be safer. There, I could flag down a police car or ask someone to call 9-1-1.

As I turned to leave, I was surprised to see a heavy-set man standing beside the concierge desk. His hair was long and kind of oily. Something about him set off alarm bells inside my head. He was partially blocking my exit. I knew better than to panic. *Stay in control, Zeke. Be cool.*

I smiled and, speaking with the best French accent I could manage, said, "Could you please to tell me where one could find zee apartment of Dr. Benton Quest?"

The man tilted his head to the side. His brow wrinkled. His ears perked up. He looked like a big puppy dog.

He looked like Xavier Dupont!

The man was about twenty-five pounds heavier and twenty-five years younger, but he had Monsieur Dupont's face.

I looked over toward the door and said, "*Un flic!*"

The man obviously understood French. His eyes grew wide. He slowly turned his head, as if he were afraid of seeing a policeman there.

Now was my chance.

As I tried to slip past him, though, he looked down at me.

I spoke loudly. *"Baal ma!"* In Wolof, that meant "excuse me."

The man stepped aside as if in reflex. He understood Wolof, too.

There was no question in my mind. It was the Greasy Man. I shot past him. Just when I thought I was going to get away, though, he grasped the back of my shirt and pulled me to a stop.

The Greasy Man spoke in his strange accent. "Where do you think you're going?"

I turned and looked at him. "Aren't you taking me to lunch?"

"Perhaps later." He smiled. Chills went down my spine. It was an evil smile. "I think we should go upstairs first." He grabbed me and picked me up.

Now it was time to panic.

I tried to break free. The Greasy Man was too strong. I started screaming for help. The Greasy Man clamped his hand over my mouth so tightly, I could barely breathe. What I did breathe wasn't good. He had a terrible case of body odor.

The Greasy Man hustled me, kicking and flailing with all my might, into the elevator. He pushed the button marked "PH". The elevator doors closed. The car began to rise.

I was in big trouble.

When the elevator reached the penthouse floor and the doors opened, I kicked at the Greasy Man with my skates. He flinched but he didn't let me go. Instead, he said, "You're only making it worse for yourself."

The Greasy Man carried me across a small vestibule and through an open door. Then we were inside what I knew must be Mrs. Winthrop's apartment. It was an enormous place filled with old furniture, white lace, and sparkling crystal. I could barely smell the lemon oil and leather polish over the stench of the Greasy Man. I looked around for Mrs. Winthrop. She was nowhere to be seen. I hoped she was okay.

I hoped Pow Wow had already finished the race. I hoped Dr. and Mrs. Gao had already called Detcctive Martino. I hoped he was already in the building now, on his way upstairs.

The Greasy Man muscled me through several rooms before pushing me into a small, dimly lit library. My skates caught on the Persian rug, and I fell to the floor. When I tried to get up, the Greasy Man planted his foot on my back and held me down.

I squirmed to watch as he reached over to the nearest shelf and tugged at one of the books – *Crime and Punishment*. The far paneled wall – that wasn't really a wall – slid to one side. Behind it stood an enormous, seven-foot-tall black stccl door with a backlit keypad and a small glowing screen set into it.

*Mrs. Winthrop's safe!* It *did* exist. Even though I was in grave dangcr, some small part of me wondered if Detective Martino had been right about the treasures that safe held. Just then, I noticed the light coming from behind the door. It was partially ajar. The safe had already been opened.

# Chapter Twenty-One

The Greasy Man picked me up by the back of my shirt, pulled me to my feet, and said, "Are you claustrophobic?"

I knew what he meant, but I shook my head and said, "I'm Zeke Armstrong. Ezekiel Tobias Armstrong." Help would arrive soon. I had to stall for time. "I know Ezekiel's kind of a weird name. All the men in my family have weird names. My dad's Nestor. Now, if your last name is Martinez, that's not all that unusual. When your last name's Armstrong, though, it's weird. You see, my dad's dad is American, but his mother's from Argentina. She named my dad. My dad's dad named my Uncle Dane. My uncle's not Danish. He's half-American, half-Argentinean, like my dad. They're brothers. Uncle

Dane's real name is Abraham. My grandfather called him "Ham" for short. When he was a boy, some of the kids at school started calling him Danish Ham, like the food. It ended up being Dane. Even though the men in my family have weird names, the women don't. My mom is Sylvie, which is a perfectly normal name if you're French, like she is. Hey, you and your dad are French, too. Isn't it a small world? My mom lived in Senegal when she was a teenager. She speaks some Wolof – a lot more than I do. Hey, by the way, where did you and your dad learn to speak Wolof?"

The Greasy Man just looked at me and frowned. "Your delay tactics will not work, Zeke Armstrong. I know who you are, and I know you're not stupid. The only thing I don't know is whether or not you're afraid of confined spaces."

I gave up the act. "Why would you care?"

"Because this will be much more enjoyable for me if you are claustrophobic." The Greasy Man used his free hand to wrench open the heavy metal door.

Where I'd expected to see treasures, I found empty shelves and some paper strewn about. A fake plastic thumb lay on the floor. Xavier Dupont had already stolen Mrs. Winthrop's money and her jewels. Suddenly it dawned on me that he must have been behind the wheel of the black Rolls Royce that almost ran me down on Fifth Avenue. It hadn't been an accident. That would also explain why the Greasy Man showed up in the lobby when he did. Xavier Dupont must have called him from the car. There was one important thing I didn't know.

"Before you throw me in there, please answer one question."

The Greasy Man frowned.

"Where's Mrs. Winthrop?"

"She's safe and mostly sound. For the time being, anyway. There is a little matter of another safe to open. *Papa* needs her for that."

Detective Martino had been right about the second safe. I looked down at the plastic thumb again. *Of course!* The small glowing screen set into the safe door was a thumbprint scanner. Even with the correct combination, that door wouldn't open unless either Mrs. Winthrop or her son placed one of their thumbs on the scanner. Xavier Dupont had obviously tried to use the fake thumb, but it didn't work. That was why he still needed Mrs. Winthrop. She must have been in the black Rolls-Royce when it zoomed past me. I could still help her. There was still time. I just had to figure out a way to get out of the jam I found myself in now.

As I tried my best to think of some new tactic, I heard someone grunt behind us.

The Greasy Man dropped me and turned around. He spoke in French. "Remy, I've told you not to sneak up on me like that."

I looked back. There stood a tall, lean blond man dressed all in green. A large black backpack was slung over his shoulder. Even though he wasn't wearing sunglasses, I knew it was the Jittery Man. I also knew that he wasn't just gesturing with his hands. He was signing. The Jittery Man – whose name was Remy – couldn't speak. He was mute. That explained why he never talked back to the Greasy Man when I found them picking through the contents of Mrs. Winthrop's purse.

I could speak French, Spanish, and English – all with no accent – and I knew a quite a few phrases in several other tongues, but I'd never learned sign language. I wished I knew what the Jittery Man was saying.

The Greasy Man obviously understood. He replied, again in French. "We're going to meet *Papa* on Roosevelt Island. From there, it's a short boat ride to a plane and the good life. First, though, we're going to put this little trouble-maker in storage."

The Jittery Man's hands moved quickly.

"It's not my problem if he runs out of air."

The Jittery Man shook his head wildly and gestured with his hands again.

The Greasy Man gave an evil laugh. "I swear, Remy. I've never understood how we could have the same father.

*They were brothers?* They looked nothing alike.

The Greasy Man continued, "Soon we'll be rich beyond our wildest dreams. What happens to this little…annoyance and that old biddy is of no consequence."

The Jittery Man gestured again.

The Greasy Man gave another evil laugh. "I'll buy you a new conscience, Remy." He tilted his head toward me. "Now, help me get rid of this headache."

The Jittery Man let the backpack slip off his shoulder. He reached inside it and pulled out a pistol. The backpack fell to the ground. The Jittery Man didn't point the gun at me. Instead, he turned it on his brother.

The Greasy Man put his hands on his hips. "Don't be a child, Remy. Put down the gun."

The Jittery Man shook his head. He was looking less creepy by the moment. Keeping the gun trained on his brother, Remy Dupont motioned for me to come to him.

Choosing sides required no thought. I tried to do as Remy Dupont asked, but the Greasy Man clenched his arm around my throat and said, "I'll finish him off right here and now if you don't drop that gun."

# Chapter Twenty-Two

As we stood there like that, the Greasy Man holding me in a chokehold and Remy Dupont holding the gun on his brother, time seemed to stand still. As scared as I was, I couldn't help but notice that the Greasy Man's body odor was getting worse. He smelled so bad, it made me sick to my stomach. I wanted to throw up.

Remy Dupont made another grunting sound.

The Greasy Man tightened his arm around my neck. I gasped for breath and tried to pull his arm away. The Greasy Man was too strong. Remy Dupont lowered the gun and dropped it to the floor.

The Greasy Man released me from his grip. Moving surprisingly fast for a man of his bulk, he snatched up the gun from the floor and pointed it at his brother. "That's fine by me, Remy. Half of a fortune is better than a third." He moved around behind his brother. "Now, both of you, get into the vault."

I didn't see that we had any choice but to do as he said. I rolled back into the cramped spaces of Mrs. Winthrop's walk-in safe. As Remy Dupont approached me, he signed something that I understood to mean, "I'm sorry."

Speaking in French, I said, "It's okay. Thanks for trying."

"Isn't that sweet?" The Greasy Man shoved his brother into the vault. "You two bleeding hearts can have all the warm and fuzzy moments you want." Keeping the gun trained on his brother and me, the Greasy Man started to close the heavy metal door. Just before it slammed shut and the lights went out, he said, "Just for the record, little brother, I never liked you."

## Chapter Twenty-Three

It was suddenly dark and quiet. For a few moments, I heard nothing but the pulse pounding in my ears. The silence didn't last long. Remy Dupont's breaths then grew loud and erratic.

I said, "Please try to stay calm. We'll use up our oxygen more quickly if we get excited. Help is on the way. Just hang in there."

His breathing grew more regular.

It would only be a matter of time before the police arrived. Once they did, though, it might be a while before they found the vault hidden in the wall in the library. We could bang on the door to let them know we were trapped inside, but I didn't know if they could get us out. Pow Wow had the prescription number, which I felt sure to be the combination, but without Mrs. Winthrop's or her son's thumbprint, the door wouldn't open. Even if they could get the fake thumb to work, it was here with us, on the floor inside the safe.

I had no idea where Mrs. Winthrop was. I had no idea if she was still alright. There was no way we could count on her getting us out. Her son, Pete, would return to New York tomorrow. I wondered if there would be enough air to last that long. It was a pretty big vault, but I doubted it was that big. I started thinking about an old black-and-white movie I'd seen in Peru, about a man who'd been buried alive. My hands started sweating. I heard the sound of loud, erratic breaths. It took a few moments for me to realize that it was me, and not Remy Dupont, who was breathing so hard.

*Get hold of yourself, Zeke!* There had to be some other way out. *Think, Zeke. Think!* Here I was, trapped inside Mrs. Winthrop's safe the way her son had been trapped inside that refrigerator. *Wait a minute...*

From what I knew about Mrs. Winthrop, I figured that there *had* to be some sort of an internal release mechanism inside the vault. At first I searched up high with my hands, and I found nothing. Then, I remembered that she was mostly concerned with kids being trapped. I looked down low. There, about three feet off the ground, I saw a glowing green button. As my eyes adjusted to the dark, the green dot grew brighter and brighter.

When I pushed the button, I heard a long tone, but nothing else happened. I drew a deep breath and let it out quickly. Just as I started looking for some other release mechanism, I heard the clicking of lock tumblers. With a whoosh and a whir, the heavy door swept open.

## Chapter Twenty-Four

Remy Dupont and I hurried out of the vault and stood in the middle of the library. I looked at him, thinking, Friend or enemy?

Even though he had stolen Mrs. Winthrop's purse, even though he had brought a snake to my room, I knew he never meant to cause anyone any serious bodily harm. When he saw Nattie Winthrop fall in the park, I could see that he was concerned about her. The gift-wrapped snake he'd given Pow Wow and me had been defanged. Most of all, though, he'd tried to save me from his own brother. I had to believe he'd decided to walk the good path.

"I know you can hear me, but I don't understand sign language. Please nod yes or no."

He nodded.

"Do you know where your father took Mrs. Winthrop?"

He nodded.

I skated to the library table and found a sheet of paper and a pen. "Can you write down the address?"

He shook his head.

"Do you know how to write?"

He frowned, took a deep breath, let it out quickly, then nodded.

"I'm sorry. I didn't mean to insult you."

He smiled. His teeth were yellowish and crooked. I forced myself not to stare at them. Instead, I smiled back. "Do you know how to get to where your father took Mrs. Winthrop?"

He nodded.

"Will you take me there?'

He nodded again.

I picked up the phone on the library table and said, "I'm going to call the police and have them meet us on Roosevelt Island."

Remy Dupont shook his head violently. He then ran over and grabbed the backpack he'd dropped on the floor. I half-expected him to pull out another gun.

He did!

Just great, I thought. *Why did I trust him?* I figured he would point the pistol at me and motion for me to put down the phone. Instead, he just stared at the firearm and shook his head. He was *smiling* at it.

Why was he smiling?

Remy Dupont emptied the ammunition clip. One single bullet dropped into his backpack. I suddenly realized that the phone I was holding had no dial tone. I dropped the receiver back into its cradle. Remy Dupont stuffed the unloaded gun into his backpack, then he pulled out a mobile phone and handed it to me. I had him use the pen and paper to write down the mobile unit's number.

As I dialed Detective Martino's number, Remy Dupont sat on the floor and pulled a pair of inline skates from his backpack. The wheel was still missing from his left skate. He yanked off his shoes and began pulling on his skates.

I got the detective's voice mail. I left a message telling him that Mrs. Winthrop was in danger, that Xavier Dupont had taken her hostage, and that he was carrying her to Roosevelt Island. I told him I didn't have the address, but that I had someone with me who could take us to the right place. I then recited the number Remy Dupont had written down and asked him to call me. When I hung up, I hoped Detective Martino would get the message quickly. More than that, though, I hoped he believed me.

Remy Dupont stood before me, inline skates on his feet, backpack over his shoulder.

I looked down at his skates and said, "We'll take a taxi. It's too far to skate."

He shook his head and motioned for me to follow him.

"Just a second." I hurried over to the safe and snatched the plastic thumb from the floor. I stuffed it in my pocket and said, "It may come in handy."

He shook his head and made some gesture that I took to mean, "It doesn't work." Then, he dashed out of the apartment and into the elevator.

I followed.

When we rolled out of the elevator on the ground floor, I saw an elderly, well-dressed couple standing at the concierge's desk. The woman looked at us and said, "Where on Earth is Reginald? Our phones are out, and we've been waiting here for–" She glanced down at our feet. Her tone became stern. "Young men, skating is strictly *verboten* in this building."

Remy Dupont ignored her. He rolled around the corner, down a short hall, and opened the door at the end. I followed to see that, inside, three uniformed men were sitting on the floor of a utility room. All had been tied up, and they all had gags in their mouths. Otherwise, they looked okay. I noticed that the wires lining one wall had been ripped from their circuits. That must have been how they took out the phones. Remy Dupont undid the closest man's gag.

The man started screaming for help. We rolled away and made our way through the lobby. I noticed my sleek black helmet on the concierge desk. As I hurried over to pluck it from the counter, the elderly couple didn't say a word. They just stood there with their mouths hanging open. As I skated away through the lobby, I said, "Oh, I think we found Reginald."

# Chapter Twenty-Five

Remy Dupont dashed across Fifth Avenue. I strapped on my helmet and followed. Roosevelt Island was east. The far side of Fifth was west. I wondered if Remy Dupont was confused. I almost said something about it, but then he tucked into a low profile and headed south. All at once, I understood. Here, where it ran alongside Central Park, the sidewalk was mostly uninterrupted all the way down to 60th Street. On the other side of Fifth Avenue, we would have had to negotiate a crosswalk every block.

Even with my new, super-fast five-wheel racing skates, I had trouble keeping up with Remy Dupont. We were flying. We zoomed past pedestrians so fast, we must have appeared to be nothing more than a couple of streaks, mine black, Remy Dupont's green. In no time, we were crossing the 72$^{nd}$ Street entrance to Central Park.

After dodging a few pedestrians, we were once again on a long stretch of sidewalk. At some point, we would surely cross Fifth Avenue again and head east. Where, I couldn't say. I had to trust that Remy Dupont knew what he was doing.

As we raced along, I heard what I thought to be the sound of inline skates behind me. I figured at first that it was just the sound of my own wheels reflecting off of the stone wall that ringed Central Park. When I jumped a small limb that had fallen down on the sidewalk, though, I could still hear the sound of skates on concrete.

I glanced back.

Pow Wow Gao was pulling into position behind me.

# Chapter Twenty-Six

I shouted over my shoulder. "How'd you find us?"

Pow Wow yelled, "I was going to Mrs. Winthrop's apartment. I saw you crossing 72$^{nd}$ when I was coming out of the park."

"How'd the race go."

"I won." Pow Wow said it without emotion. It was just a statement of fact.

"Congratulations."

"Thanks."

"Where are your parents?"

"Couldn't find them." Pow Wow pulled in closer. "Hey, what are we doing?"

"Going to Roosevelt Island to save Mrs. Winthrop."

Most of the guys I knew at school would have been shocked by a statement like that, or they would have accused me of kidding around. Pow Wow had been hanging out with me too long. All he said was, "Who's that up ahead?"

"Remy Dupont."

"Who's he?"

"Monsieur Dupont's son. You know, the guy who stole Mrs. Winthrop's purse and brought us that snake. He can't talk. He just saved my life."

Pow Wow was so stunned, he didn't say anything else until we reached 60$^{th}$ Street.

As we played follow-the-leader, zigzagging through the yellow taxis and the other cars caught in traffic on Fifth Avenue, I called ahead, "Are you sure we shouldn't take a cab?"

Remy Dupont nodded.

"Wouldn't a car would be faster?"

He shook his head then gestured with his hands.

Pow Wow called out, "There's too much traffic on the bridge."

Remy Dupont looked back at him.

I looked back at him. "How do you know that, Pow Wow?"

He pointed at Remy Dupont. "I'm just repeating what he said."

Remy Dupont smiled and gestured again.

Pow Wow didn't gesture. He just spoke. "I'm Richard Gao. Everybody calls me Pow Wow. Nice to meet you, too."

Now it was my turn to be stunned. I was used to being the kid with the mysterious past, the kid with the hidden talent. After all the time I'd known Pow Wow, after all the times he'd heard me speaking to people in French or in Spanish, he'd never once mentioned that he could talk to people who couldn't talk.

As we headed east on 59th Street, I was finally able to ask him, "Where'd you learn sign language?"

"From my cousin Alex. He's mute, too. He lived next door when we were little kids."

Even though all I said in reply was, "Cool," what I really meant was, *I have a whole new respect for you.* Somehow, I think Pow Wow understood that, because I glanced back to see a strange smile on his face. It looked like he was embarrassed.

I explained everything to Pow Wow as we raced across town. In places where the sidewalk became crowded, we jumped off and skated fast on asphalt. 59$^{th}$ was a one-way street. The traffic flowed west, heading toward us. It was a lot easier to dodge oncoming cars than it was to worry about them sneaking up behind you.

As we crossed Park Avenue, I couldn't help but notice the swath of bright-yellow flowers filling the median. Uncle Dane told me once what they were. I seem to remember him saying they were tulips, but I couldn't be sure. I wondered how you said "tulip" in sign language. A moment later, I wondered why I had such strange thoughts at such tense times.

# Chapter Twenty-Seven

As we neared Second Avenue, we came to a broad, brick-paved plaza. A few small trees dotted the perimeter. At the far end of the plaza stood an unusual-looking, two-story structure. Remy Dupont gestured with his hands then sprinted toward it.

I pointed at the Queensboro Bridge and said, "Hey, aren't we going that way?"

He just kept skating.

"Come on, Zeke. He says we have to hurry." Pow Wow dashed after him.

I quickly followed.

The next thing I knew, I was skating under a sign that read: *Entrance*. I then found myself crab-walking up an open-air set of concrete steps. Climbing stairs in inline skates is a stupid thing to do. Under normal circumstances, I wouldn't have ever attempted anything that risky. These weren't normal circumstances. Mrs. Winthrop was in danger. The only thing I couldn't figure out was why saving Mrs. Winthrop on Roosevelt Island meant climbing to the second floor of a building at 59th Street and Second Avenue in Manhattan.

When we reached the top of the stairs, I understood. My stomach fell to my knees. I could almost hear Mrs. Gao's tour-guide voice: *The Roosevelt Island Tram is the only aerial commuter tramway in North America. Each of its two gondola cabins carries up to 125 passengers and travels a distance of 3,100 feet at an average speed of sixteen miles per hour in four and a half minutes. The gondolas rise to 250 feet and travel at certain points parallel to and slightly higher than the adjacent Queensboro Bridge.*

Remy Dupont passed some money through the ticket window and held up three fingers. He grabbed the tokens the man in the booth gave him, then passed one of each to Pow Wow and me. Remy

Dupont went through the turnstile without taking his change. Pow Wow and I followed him onto the open concrete loading platform.

The big gondola cabin with its tall, 360-degree windows was parked there, doors open. A few people with bicycles and tennis rackets milled around inside. Overhead, two sets of cables rose in a graceful arc to the first of the tram's towers. I felt sick to my stomach. That wasn't even the tall tower. A voice came over the loudspeaker. The gondola would be leaving in a matter of moments.

Remy Dupont rolled into the cabin. Pow Wow followed him inside. I knew I had to do the same, but it seemed as if my wheels were frozen to the concrete platform. An announcement came over the loudspeaker. The cabin doors were closing.

My worst nightmare was coming true.

# Chapter Twenty-Eight

Pow Wow stood just inside the cabin doors yelling, "Come on!"

Remy Dupont motioned me inside.

Mrs. Winthrop's in danger, I told myself. *Do this for her.* I took a deep breath, rolled across the platform, then stepped into the cabin between Remy Dupont and Pow Wow Gao. I turned around as the doors slid shut behind me. Remy Dupont reached up and grasped the metal grip bar running overhead. With my inline skates on, I was just tall enough to reach it, too.

I clenched my hand around the bar and shut my eyes tight.

With an electrostatic whine and a strong rocking motion, the gondola started moving. At first, it wasn't so bad. It felt like we were in a cross-town bus lurching forward in traffic. We didn't seem to be going any higher.

That quickly changed.

The cabin began to rise. Seeing how high we were would be bad. Not seeing was worse. Looking down at my feet, I opened my eyes. Remy Dupont's skates were to my right. Pow Wow's skates were to my left. I looked over at Pow Wow, intending to focus on his face. Even so, I saw that we were gliding higher and higher above the buildings and the city streets. My stomach dropped from my knees to my ankles.

I said, "I don't feel so good."

Pow Wow looked at me. A moment later, he had that *Oh,* now *I understand* look on his face. He spoke to Remy Dupont. "Zeke's scared of aerial trams."

I didn't look back, but I assumed Remy Dupont was signing something. I must have been right, because Pow Wow then said, "No, he's not afraid of heights or confined spaces. He even likes chairlifts. He *likes* them. For some reason, though, gondolas give him the creeps."

After waiting a few moments for Remy Dupont to sign something else, Pow Wow nodded and said, "I know it doesn't make any sense."

Great, I thought sarcastically. There I was, living out my worst nightmare while my best friend discussed my lack of logic with the man who'd sent a timber rattlesnake to our room. The situation was, as Uncle Dane would say, "surreal."

A moment later, I thought of Mrs. Winthrop again. She was in trouble. We had to help her. I had to get through this for her. I faced the window and looked out. Even though we were moving higher and higher over the city, I forced myself to think about Nattie Winthrop and how we best could help her.

*Why haven't I heard back from Detective Martino?* I decided to try him once more before making a call to 9-1-1. We needed the police to meet us when we reached the tram station on Roosevelt Island.

I pulled Remy Dupont's mobile phone from my pocket. I looked at the unit. Somehow it had turned itself off. That was why the detective hadn't called – he hadn't been able to. I hit the power button.

While waiting for the unit to boot up, I took a deep breath to calm myself. Instead, it sent chills down my spine. Even before the gun barrel pressed against my back, even before I heard the words spoken in that strange accent, I knew the Greasy Man was approaching me from behind. I could smell him from three feet away.

# Chapter Twenty-Nine

"It would appear that we have a couple of Houdinis here." The Greasy Man spoke in French. "Don't make any sudden moves, any of you. That includes your Asian friend."

Pow Wow leaned over and whispered, "Hey, Zeke. What's that guy saying?"

"He's telling us not to make any sudden moves."

"Huh?"

Looking straight ahead, I saw that we were now ascending across the East River. Being in a gondola over open water was even worse than being in a gondola over hard pavement. Together with the

Greasy Man's stench, I didn't think I'd be able to hold down my breakfast much longer.

Pow Wow elbowed me. "What's going on, Zeke?"

"The man behind me is Remy Dupont's brother. He's pressing a gun into my back."

Out of the corner of my eye, I could see Remy Dupont making gestures with the hand he'd placed on the overhead grip bar. Pow Wow was watching him. I wondered what he was saying.

The Greasy Man put his mouth between Pow Wow's and my ear and spoke softly in English. "Nobody moves. No funny stuff. I won't hesitate to use the gun I have pressed into young Mr. Armstrong's back." His breath was foul.

Pow Wow said, "Pee-yew!" then turned and backed away. "Man, don't you ever shower or brush your teeth?"

I was stunned speechless. Again.

Pow Wow spoke in a loud voice. "Everyone, may I have your attention, please?"

The interior of the cabin fell quiet. All I could hear was the buffeting of the wind and the creaking of the cables. What was Pow Wow up to?

He pointed at Remy Dupont's brother. "That man is holding a gun against my friend Zeke's back." An audible gasp filled the cabin. Pow Wow spoke even louder. "That man wants to hurt my friend. The thing is, he can't. He doesn't realize that he's holding a fake gun."

The Greasy Man held up the pistol and inspected it. From the look on his face, I knew Pow Wow was right. It *was* a fake gun. Remy Dupont must have signed the information to Pow Wow when the Greasy Man was breathing on me. That explained why Remy Dupont laughed when he pulled the second gun out of his backpack at Nattie Winthrop's apartment. He'd just figured out that the Greasy Man forced us into the safe with a fake gun.

Pow Wow looked at the tram operator and said, "Would you please call the police and have them meet us on Roosevelt Island? Meanwhile, we could use a little help keeping this man from moving about the cabin."

A couple of the bigger men on board tackled the stunned Greasy Man and held him to the ground. The tram operator spoke into a microphone and asked the person at the other end of the line for police assistance. Pow Wow stood there, looking pretty pleased with himself, but it didn't last long.

Remy Dupont dropped his backpack and pulled out a gun. The *real* gun. It was a good thing he'd unloaded it back at Mrs. Winthrop's apartment.

The problem was, the Greasy Man didn't know the gun wasn't loaded. He obviously thought his brother was going to shoot him, because he began thrashing about like a wild animal. He quickly broke free from the men holding him. As he stormed through the gondola, he first tried to pry apart the sliding cabin doors, but they were locked tight. He looked all around, then he looked up. He dashed down the cabin, came to an abrupt stop, then reached overhead and pulled. One end of a ladder popped free. The Greasy Man quickly lowered it to the floor and began to climb. At the top of the ladder was a skylight – a skylight that I knew must open onto the roof of the gondola.

I pushed Pow Wow back against the wall. As we stood there, watching, not knowing what to do, Remy Dupont searched frantically through his backpack. *What is he looking for?* All at once, I remembered him dropping the single bullet into his pack. He was going to load the gun. Would he really try to shoot his brother?

The tram operator shouted for everyone to hold tight. The gondola came to an abrupt stop. As the cabin heaved back and forth, Pow Wow and I struggled to remain upright on our skates. Remy Dupont lost his balance and fell. The contents of his backpack spilled. A single bullet skittered across the floor into the corner.

The gondola kept rocking.

The Greasy Man kept climbing. The men who'd held him down at first tried to grab his legs and pull him from the ladder. He kicked at them. Both men came away with a bloody noses.

The gondola kept rocking.

Remy Dupont kicked off his skates, doffed his helmet, and jammed the pistol under the belt that held up his shorts. He then dove into the corner of the cabin. On hands and knees, he searched for the missing bullet.

The gondola kept rocking.

There was a banging sound from above. I looked up to see the Greasy Man punching at the skylight with his fist. Moments later, it popped open. He began to climb up through the narrow hole.

The gondola was rocking less, now.

Remy Dupont stood and braced himself in corner of the cabin. Even though I couldn't see it, I assumed he'd found the bullet, because he popped out the clip, inserted something into it, then reassembled the gun. When he looked up the ladder, though, his brother was already out of sight. He again stuffed the gun under his belt, then he hurried to the bottom of the ladder and started to climb.

All the people in the cabin stood stunned. Even the tram operator didn't move. Nobody was going to do anything.

It was up to me. I hurried to the back side of the ladder and looked up at Remy Dupont through the rungs. "Don't do anything stupid. They'll put you away for a long, long time. He's not worth it."

He took another step.

"I'll tell the police how you helped me. I'll tell them how you tried to help Mrs. Winthrop. I'll ask them to take it easy on you. Just let him go."

Remy Dupont looked down at me for a moment. He then took the pistol from under his belt. Grasping the ladder with both arms, he snapped out the clip and sent the single bullet bouncing across the floor again. He then popped the clip back in and handed me the pistol. I dropped it to the floor beside the fake gun as he scurried up the ladder.

I kicked off my skates, got rid of my helmet, and started to climb.

Pow Wow rolled over and pulled me to a stop. "What are you doing?"

"I'm going up there. I have to try to talk him out of doing something stupid."

"I can't just stand here and let you do that."

I started climbing again. "I don't want you to stand there. I want you to get up here and hold my feet." In the corner of my eye, I could see Pow Wow removing his skates and helmet.

Moments later, I was looking out across the top deck of the gondola. Remy Dupont stood with his back to me. His brother was facing him. They were about three feet apart. The wind was blowing hard. A strong gust could send one or both of them over the edge. It was a long fall from there. Traffic blared past on the Queensboro Bridge. The skyscrapers of New York sprouted up in the background like the hoodoos at Bryce Canyon.

I felt Pow Wow's arm wrap around my ankles. Overhead, the cables moaned. The pulleys and the mechanism that kept the gondola attached to the cables creaked and complained. I found nothing reassuring about that.

Remy Dupont held his hands in front of him and signed something to his brother. Even if Pow Wow had been there to translate, he couldn't have seen what Remy Dupont said.

The Greasy Man made a mocking face and said, "Oh boohoo, Remy. You never had the stomach to be a Dupont. I'll never know why *Papa* had to bring you along."

I couldn't be sure what Remy Dupont signed at that point, but it obviously made the Greasy Man angry. He charged at his brother. The two of them locked arms and began to scuffle. It was hard to watch as they shoved each other around on top of the gondola. One wrong step and one – or both – of them would fall over the edge. It was a long way down to the East River.

The Greasy Man broke free and punched his brother in the face. The blow sent Remy Dupont reeling. The heels of his sock-covered feet banged into the low railing that ran around the outside edge of the gondola's roof. Remy Dupont leaned back. His arms gyrated like the blades of a Dutch windmill. I was so afraid he might fall, I could barely keep my eyes open.

Just as I felt sure he was going to topple over backwards, though, Remy Dupont regained his balance and charged forward. He shoved his brother back, back, back. All at once, I realized that their feet were coming straight for my head. I ducked down into the skylight.

Moments later, I heard screams coming from inside the cabin. I poked my head up out of the skylight. I didn't see Remy Dupont or the Greasy Man.

My heart sank. I looked down at Pow Wow and said, "Did they fall?"

He glanced around, then he looked back up at me. "No. They're hanging off the side."

I looked across the top of the gondola and saw four hands gripping the far railing.

Over the roar of the wind, I heard the Greasy Man yell, "Help! I can't hold on!"

I looked down at Pow Wow. "Let go of my ankles."

"What are you doing?"

"I'm going to help Remy."

"Zeke, don't do anything stu–"

"He saved my life, and he's the only one who can take us to Mrs. Winthrop."

Pow Wow let go. I scurried up the ladder. Next thing I knew, I was rushing across the top of the gondola. The wind blew hard. I could see the river stretch out far below me. I was looking down on the traffic that crossed the Queensboro Bridge. I stood above the tops of many of the tall buildings in Manhattan. I barely noticed.

As I lay down flat on the top of the cabin and grasped Remy Dupont's wrists, I felt someone grab hold of my ankles. I looked down to see Pow Wow lying there.

He said, "Gotcha!"

I asked, "Who's got you?"

He glanced down. "Everybody."

"Alright, then. Let's pull."

Slowly but sure, we managed to pull Remy Dupont up onto the top of the gondola. While we all continued to lay on our stomachs, he stood and looked down at his brother's fingers.

I called out, "Remy! Grab him!"

He looked back at me. The wind suddenly gusted, and he had to take a side step to keep from being blown over.

"You can't let him die like this."

Remy Dupont looked at his brother's fingers again, then he nodded.

Hoping he meant he agreed with me, and not that he *could* let the Greasy Man fall, I said, "Lie down flat. I'll grab your ankles. Pow Wow's got mine. We'll make another chain."

He nodded and, as if suddenly awake after a long sleep, he sprang to action.

Once he was in position, I screamed, "Ready!"

Remy Dupont grabbed his brother's wrists and began to pull. Slowly but surely, our chain worked. First Pow Wow, then me, then Remy Dupont, then finally the Greasy Man, we all made our way back through the skylight and down the stairs.

Four of the men on board held the Greasy Man. He stood there, head hung low, and said, "Brother? Can you ever forgive me?"

Remy Dupont's nose was all bloody from where the Greasy Man had hit him. Tomorrow, he would have a big black eye. He faced his brother, seemed to consider his words, then he turned to walk away. At that point, the Greasy Man lurched forward and broke free from the men holding him. He dove to the floor, grabbed something, then was suddenly on his feet again. He was holding a gun in each hand. One was a fake, but the other was real. He pointed the weapons at the back of his brother's head and pulled the triggers. There was a small click. The Greasy Man looked astounded that at least one of the guns hadn't fired.

Remy Dupont turned around. He punched his brother in the face so hard, it hurt to hear. The Greasy Man hit the ground, unconscious. Everyone on board applauded.

As the tram started moving again, I looked out over the East River. Manhattan rose from one bank, Roosevelt Island from the other. It was a beautiful sight. I suddenly realized that I was no longer afraid of gondolas. All it had taken was a near-death experience.

## Chapter Thirty

When the tram reached its dock on Roosevelt Island, Detective Martino was waiting for us. I gave him a quick explanation of what had happened and told him that Mrs. Winthrop was still in danger. While the Greasy Man was taken away in a police ambulance, the detective and Remy Dupont had a brief conversation – with Pow Wow's help.

Moments later, the detective barked, "Let's move 'em out!" Pow Wow and I piled into the front seat of an unmarked car. Detective Martino locked Remy Dupont in the back, then he got behind the wheel and gunned the engine.

Remy Dupont gave directions. Pow Wow told the detective what he was saying. We raced through the streets with a string of police cars behind us. It was a strange thing to think, but the procession of automobiles reminded me of a long line of inline skaters, one drafting behind the other.

Four minutes later, we came to an abrupt stop in front of a modern apartment building. A black Rolls Royce was backed in near a side entrance. I said, "That's the car Monsieur Dupont was driving."

Remy Dupont signed something to Pow Wow.

Pow Wow turned to Detective Martino. "The side apartment on the lower level." He pointed at the black Rolls-Royce. "The one next to that car."

As a uniformed officer came to handcuff Remy Dupont and take him away, I said goodbye, thanked him, and told him I'd tell the authorities how he'd helped. Pow Wow told him to take care of himself. Remy Dupont signed something with his cuffed hands, then he went with the policeman.

"What'd he say?"

Pow Wow nodded and said, "He said we restored his faith in humanity."

"Really?"

Pow Wow bit his lower lip. "I think so. Either that, or he told me to stop feeding the blue cat. It was hard to tell with the handcuffs on."

Another uniformed officer approached the driver's door of our unmarked car. Detective Martino told us the policeman – his name was Officer Wilson – would take care of us. We all got out, and the detective put us in the back seat of the car. Officer Wilson got behind the wheel. Detective Martino walked away with a group of other men toward the front of the apartment building, Officer Wilson started the car and drove us around the block. He said he was going to get us "out of the line of fire."

After a few minutes of sitting there, wondering what was happening, I heard what I thought to be Detective Martino's voice crackle over the police radio. "Bring 'em back, Wilson."

As we approached the apartment building the second time, I saw a squad car driving away. Monsieur Dupont was in the back seat. He looked over at me as we passed. I wanted to stick out my tongue at him, but I decided it'd be more mature to ignore him.

There were now a dozen police cars parked in front of the building. Uniformed officers were posted all around the building. Four policemen stood guard around the black Rolls Royce.

Officer Wilson unlocked our car doors. Detective Martino slipped into the back seat and said, "We have a bit of a situation here. Zeke, just how did you get yourself out of that vault in Mrs. Winthrop's apartment?"

I ran through the details of how, after my eyes adjusted to the dark, I'd been able to see the glowing green button.

He frowned. "Well, it would seem that Mr. Dupont has put poor Mrs. Winthrop inside the vault and disabled its interior release."

"How do you know that?"

"Because he told us he did…just before he forgot how to speak English. If only we had the combination to the safe…"

"I know the combination."

Pow Wow and I were hustled inside the apartment, through a hidden panel, and down a small stairway before I had a chance tell Officer Martino that the combination alone wouldn't be enough.

A persistent beep echoed from the concrete walls of the small basement room. There, on a table near the stairs stood a prescription bottle – with the label removed. Detective Martino told us that Monsieur Dupont had swallowed it. Nearby lay the source of the beep – a small, disc-shaped metallic device. It was Mrs. Winthrop's medication reminder.

Detective Martino pointed out the safe door, on the far side of the room. It appeared identical to the one in Mrs. Winthrop's Fifth Avenue apartment. The detective said, "What's the combination?"

"It's not going to do you any good."

He looked at me. "What do you mean, Zeke?"

I pointed out the small glowing screen and explained how either Mrs. Winthrop's or her son's thumbprint was needed to open the vault.

Detective Martino said, "Her son is due back tomorrow morning." He looked past me and said, "Jenkins, get the manufacturer on the phone and see if she'll have enough oxygen to last until morning."

I said, "Even if she has enough air, she doesn't have that much time."

The detective looked at me. "What?"

I pointed at the label-less prescription bottle on the table. "She has to take one of those capsules every eight hours. Hear that beep?"

He nodded.

"She's due for a dose now."

It all seemed hopeless. Poor Mrs. Winthrop. After all the times she'd warned kids about getting trapped in old refrigerators, it seemed that she had become trapped in one herself. I could only imagine how terrified she must have been. I remembered how it felt to be locked inside that vault, if only for a few minutes. The thought of never getting out was awful. I became so nervous, my hands once again started sweating. When I reached down to dry them off on my shorts, I felt something in my pocket.

Uncle Dane was always saying, "Hope springs eternal." I'd never really understood what he meant by that…until now.

# Chapter Thirty-One

I pulled out the artificial thumb. On one side was a series of irregular, interlocking ridges. Mrs. Winthrop's thumbprint, I guessed. I wondered for a moment how Xavier Dupont had gotten the print and had it molded into this piece of plastic, but I didn't have time to think about it now.

As I approached the safe, one of the other policemen tried to stop me. Detective Martino held him back. I punched in the code as I remembered it, 782051263, then held the ridged part of the fake thumb against the scanner. Nothing. I tried holding the thumb on the screen while trying the combination again. Still, nothing. Finally, I tried holding the thumb up to the screen, then taking it away before punching in the long string of numbers. *Nada.*

Detective Martino said, "Are you sure you're punching in the right numbers?"

I nodded. The combination was right, but something else was wrong. Xavier Dupont had obviously discarded the fake thumb at Mrs. Winthrop's Fifth Avenue apartment because it didn't work. If it didn't work there, why would it work here?

Hopeless, I thought.

My hands got all sweaty again. As I started drying them off on my shorts, it suddenly occurred to me that that's what thumbs were. Sweaty. Even when your hands were dry, there was still some moisture in your skin. That's what made some touch-sensitive switches work – moisture. I remembered the lamp in Pow Wow's and my room. I thought about how I'd gotten it to switch on and off with the damp washcloth. I wondered if…

Once again, I slowly and carefully punched in the code. I rubbed the ridged part of the fake thumb into the palm of my sweaty hand. Taking a deep breath, I held it against the small glowing screen. A long tone sounded from the door.

## Chapter Thirty-Two

Mrs. Gao was so happy to be sitting there in the middle of the Crystal Room at Tavern on the Green, she just about glowed. No matter what had happened during the day, she was living a dream come true this evening. Dr. Gao looked happy, too. I think he was just relieved that his son was safe, and that he would be able to return me to my parents and my uncle undamaged.

After Detective Martino took Pow Wow and me back to the Gaos, we'd learned that they were helping a man who'd had an epileptic seizure when Pow Wow won the Big Apple Inline Skate-Off. Mrs. Gao had been watching the time, but Pow Wow crossed the finish line a full five minutes before either she or Dr. Gao expected him to. When Mrs. Gao learned the truth about Xavier Dupont, she said she knew he was up to no good. I asked how she knew. She said her *yeye* – her father's father – told her once that you could tell everything you needed to know about a man from his shoes. Since she seemed to be in a mood for explaining things, I asked how she'd known the names of the New York Public Library lions. She just smiled and said that women sometimes needed to keep their "air of mystery."

Chandeliers twinkled overhead. Nighttime views of Tavern on the Green's gardens filled the large windows that surrounded the dining room. Pow Wow and I were wearing our coats and ties again. This time, neither of us complained about having to put them on. Nattie Winthrop sat there between us at the special, large table that she'd arranged for the occasion. Even after all she'd been through, even though she now had two bandages on her forehead, she looked good. Her hair was fixed up, and she was wearing a new dress and a new pair of glasses. She still smelled like talcum powder. When I asked her why she'd kept that vault on Roosevelt Island, she told me that the apartment building had been constructed on the site of her childhood home.

There were three empty chairs next to me. One for my mom, one for my dad, one for Uncle Dane. My parents would be arriving any minute now. I could hardly wait. Uncle Dane would be a bit late, he said.

Detective Paul Martino was sitting on the opposite side of the table with Emily Mars, the pretty, auburn-haired herpetologist. On our way into the restaurant, the detective kept thanking Pow Wow and me for bringing them together. We told him he should thank Remy Dupont or, at least, the snake. Detective Martino said he didn't care much for snakes, but that he would do what he could for Remy. As it turned out, Ms. Mars knew Remy Dupont from the time she'd spent in Senegal studying *Dendroaspis polylepis* – a snake known as the black mamba. Remy was one of her field assistants, and he'd been an excellent snake handler. She'd heard that his brother – the Greasy Man's name was Bruno Dupont – and his father were outlaws in Senegal. The two of them had been investigated on charges of tampering with a Dakar company's fingerprint identification system, but they'd fled the country before they could be brought to trial. No matter what she thought of Monsieur Dupont and the Greasy Man, though, Ms. Mars liked Remy very much. She said she'd be glad to vouch for his character.

The detective and Emily Mars weren't the only ones who were going to try to help Remy Dupont. Because he'd tried to save my life and had given himself up to the authorities in order to help her, Mrs. Winthrop had hired a good attorney to represent him as he face the consequences of what he'd done. Me, I planned to make good on my promise to tell the authorities everything he'd done for me and Mrs. Winthrop.

Things weren't looking so good for Xavier Dupont and the Greasy Man. Both were facing attempted murder charges, not to mention prosecution for a long list of other crimes. As I suspected, Monsieur Dupont was a con man. He'd used the money he'd swindled from a retirement fund to finance the trip to New York so he could find Nattie Winthrop. He waited for her son to leave the country, then he put his plan in action.

If he'd gotten away with it, Monsieur Dupont and the Greasy Man would have stolen enough cash and precious gems to finance Health for the World for another decade. Because I'd helped to foil their plot, Health for the World *would* now be financed for another decade. When my parents arrived, Mrs. Winthrop was going to present them with a check that would keep the organization's projects alive for at least another ten years. As sad as I was to know Mom and Dad wouldn't be coming to live in Dallas, I was mostly happy to know they could be able to continue their work in India. Besides, it wasn't so bad living with Uncle Dane, and I'd still get to see my folks three or four times a year.

The maitre d' came to the table and said that Mr. Armstrong had a visitor. It took a moment for me to realize that he meant me. When I turned around and looked back at the doorway, I expected to see Mom, Dad, or Uncle Dane.

Instead, there was a tall, lean man with very dark skin standing there. It was Ahmedou Diop, the cab driver who'd helped me follow Remy Dupont after he'd stolen Mrs. Winthrop's purse. I'd almost forgotten asking him to come by. I got up and hurried over to him. In my pocket was an envelope containing ten times the amount of money I owed him for cab fare. Uncle Dane had told me over the phone that he thought it was the right thing to do. When I pulled out the envelope and passed it to Monsieur Diop, I said, "*Jërë jëf.*"

For a moment, he seemed shocked to hear me speak in Wolof. He then smiled a bright smile and replied, "You're welcome."

I returned to our table and sat talking with Mrs. Winthrop and Pow Wow. Mrs. Gao giggled and Dr. Gao laughed softly. Detective Martino told a lot of jokes, and he kept using the word "supposably."

Emily Mars didn't seem to care. She just smiled. The people at the table next to ours made a toast and clinked glasses.

Just as I thought how happy everyone seemed, just as I thought how happy I'd be once my parents arrived, Mrs. Gao suddenly stood and said, "Nestor! Sylvie! How lovely it is to see you again."

I felt a woman's hand on one shoulder, and a man's hand on my other. Before I turned around, I smiled and said, "Mrs. Winthrop, I'd like to introduce you to my mom and dad."

The End

**Coming soon.**

**The third Zeke Armstrong Mystery**

## *White Out*

Zeke Armstrong and Pow Wow Gao are bored stiff in a snowboarder's paradise. With their parents in India helping out after an earthquake, the boys have gone to stay with Zeke's grandmother, an elderly woman who sits in her Alpine chalet doing needlepoint all day. Zeke's eleven-year-old cousin, Zoë, is an ace snowboarder, but she spends most of her time at the chalet studying for an exam. Zeke and Pow Wow would give almost anything for a little excitement, but they soon learn why people say, "Be careful what you wish for..." In the middle of the night, Zeke's grandmother wakes the boys and Zoë to send them on a snowboarding dash down the mountain, followed by a perilous trek across the French countryside. When they reach Paris, Zeke learns that his grandmother has a big secret. She also has information that, if it falls into the wrong hands, could put hundreds of innocent people in danger. Zeke, Pow Wow, and Zoë must push their snowboarding skills to the limit to keep the information safe. Will they make it in time?